Front cover – designed by Author with the use of Canva

Illustrators – Karen Webb

We Could be Heroes

Heroes

(Lucas's Story)

For Lucas, Rosienna & Maverick

Thank you for being an inspiration & for letting me write you your own story

Remember to dream big little ones.

Love always

xxx

Chapter One
Pickle Lane

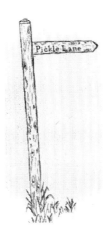

On the edge of a small, old town not at all too far from here, where the people were all super friendly - sometimes oddly friendly if you ask me, - and everyone knew all about each other. In a place where the sunrises in the west and sets in the east, and where all the houses were big, fancy, detached, and all pretty much the same……. all apart from the gardens, that is. Yes, I would say they were all slightly different. You see people in this little town liked to try and outdo one another, and every year this little town held a competition for the best garden in the neighbourhood. You could say that this is the type of place where not an awful lot really happens, the people here are all nice and pleasant…. but there were the odd few that had their secrets…. and in this odd little town is where our story begins.

Our story starts with four heroes playing in a little park. What makes them heroes I hear you ask?.... Well….if you keep reading you'll find out, won't you…..

Now, this park is just down the road from the large house in which our heroes all live, with one another and their loved ones. This house did indeed look the exact same as everyone else's in the street and the only thing telling them apart were the numbers above the doors and their gardens, yes they were all the same size but some of them had beautiful flower beds, others had herbs and bushes, and some people had all different stunning fruit and blossom trees that always smelt amazing when you passed, as well as them having all different-sized quirky swimming pools too.

Let us get back to our heroes, I think we'll start with the youngest of the four…yes that seems to be a good place to start….

Maverick, a smiley, red-haired, blue-eyed, boy, that we find absolutely covered head to toe in mud, happily smiling as he plays on the big, tall, twisty, red slide that of course has the big puddle at the bottom, in which he loves splashing in... Well he's actually seeing if he can miss it every time he slides down but keeps falling into it laughing every time he does.

Next, we find Rosienna, a beautiful blonde girl in a pretty frilly blue dress, her hair falling neatly around her shoulders as her blue eyes sparkle in the sunlight that has just reappeared from behind the clouds once more, You'll find her on the swings, swinging as high as she can, she's a very gentle young lady that has a great love of animals and she loves to read too, but she's nobody's fool, and will happily take charge of these boys.

Now we can spot Conor, a tall boy, who's the oldest of the four, he has the most piercing blue eyes and white-blonde hair, and he's definitely the joker of the group, but he always has the attitude of if you see someone without a smile, give them yours. Conor is extremely clever, he loves history and space, and he is currently pretending that the climbing frame is a huge Rocketship that's about to head off in the direction of Mars.

And last but not at all least is little Lucas who is the second eldest and has the best imagination, he loves nothing more than to play with his friends and he loves to play pretend, he is short in height, with a cute round face, brown scruffy hair, and deep blue eyes, but don't be fooled by his cute dimpled smile and height boys and girls, this little boy can sometimes be very cheeky, but he's currently casually running around chasing his football, that he's just kicked towards Conor and his "Rocketship".

You see our heroes are all very close, not only in age, I mean although they're Six, Seven, Eight and Nine, they are also pretty close, you see our heroes have all grown up together and they like to play a lot of fun and interesting games.... sometimes they're school teachers and pupils carrying their school bags around the house and intently listening to one another, sometimes they're dinosaurs and explorers, other times there fairy's that attend the most fabulous tea parties and summer balls, sometimes they're pirates that sail the high seas and like to walk the plank, and on the odd occasion they are spacemen and women that get sucked through to different and dark, strange planets where they meet the weirdest creatures, but each game is different and they always have the best time in the world of their imagination.

Now back to our heroes, who spend just a short while longer at the park, When it starts to become rather cold, cloudy, and windy, and I get the impression it might rain cats and dogs.... No, really... it might actually rain cats and dogs. They decide that they'd better not chance it, Nana Sharon might be worried if they all come back home wet and cold.

Now Nana Sharon was the best Nana our heroes could ever wish for, she always got involved with their games, and she liked to spend time with our heroes but one important thing is she was always there for our heroes, whenever they needed her, day or night and she loves these heroes millions.

Nana Sharon is the cuddliest woman you've ever met, she always greeted you with a smile and a warm hug, her long blonde hair was silky soft and her round glasses perched on the top of her nose. Our heroes know she's always there should they need her, even if it were for the smallest of things like toilet paper to be bought into the bathroom or to play a game with them and sometimes, it could just even be for a snuggle, she told the best stories…. no one ever told stories the way Nana Sharon did, she always made the places sound so real and she always did the voices of the characters to make them sound real too, Our heroes would sit for hours just listening to her.

But let's get back to our heroes………..for now.

"I think we better head home, it looks like it'll rain," Rosienna calls over to the boys

"That sounds like it might be a good idea," Conor tells her as he also looks at the darkening sky above them and they all agree to leave the park and head home.

They begin to walk towards the street where you can find their house but as they get halfway down the street, the sun starts to shine once more…. but weirdly…. only more on the right-hand side of the street. They cross over the road so that there following the sun, they can feel its warmth on their skin, but suddenly it moves again…. and they notice it's now down the end of "Pickle Lane" which is a place that they know they're not supposed to go (Now Nana had told them more than once, that they shouldn't go down there, that it's a weird, scary, and dark place to go and that it would be extremely dangerous for them to go anywhere near "Pickle Lane". She had mentioned once or twice that strange and mysterious things happen there and that people have been known to go missing when heading down Pickle Lane…but that's just a story to scare young children away…Right?…..hang on….or is it?

At the end of Pickle Lane, they spot something that is weirdly colourful and that's when our heroes notice that it's a large bunch of multi-coloured balloons….No, wait a minute, it can't be… there are never balloons around Parker Drive, the town council banned them years ago after the townspeople released hundreds of balloons and lots of birds flew into them.

"Let's go this way!!" Maverick suggests as he points down Pickle Lane "Look at all those Balloons!!!....I like balloons and it's been so long since I've been able to have one" he says as he continues pointing in their direction and they all start to enter.

Now Pickle Lane had all these stories to keep people out and away, but no one actually knows what's at the other end of Pickle Lane….. or that's what we thought anyway……

Pickle lane had always looked uninviting and rather scary or so our heroes had thought, the hedges were very high and prickly, and the trees were overgrown and overlooked the lane so it appeared quite dark and dingy within a tunnel of trees, the smell was a mixture of fish and smelly old socks, the path beneath their feet is uneven and muddy, and there were no flowers or anything green or pretty insight, nothing apart from the sun shining brightly at the end of the lane, and of course and the large bundle of multi-coloured balloons. When our heroes get halfway down the lane, they start to hear some weird noises, dogs barking, a loud bang that's come from somewhere, a sound that kind of sounded like it was an old sports car that was backfiring, they can hear a weird laugh from somewhere too, as well as some weird rustling sound that they can hear just behind them, that kind of spooks them.

"I don't like it, I don't like it," Lucas says as they walk a little further down and into Pickle lane, that's when they hear more of a growling noise "We should have gone the other way, Maybe we should go back," he tells his friends in a panicked tone

"It's okay Lucas, be brave," Rosienna tells him but something sounds like it's rustling in the hedge just beside her and she swiftly takes Lucas's hand and moves forward as the rustling becomes louder than before "I do hope that's nothing scary," she says aloud

"It might be a ghost," Conor says and no one can tell if he's being serious or not

Rosienna shoots Conor a look as if to say don't be ridiculous

"What?" he says "It could be"

"Don't be so silly!, there's nothing in parker drive that can hurt us," she tells him "C'mon we're nearly at the end," and she takes Lucas's hand again and marches forward some more.

Suddenly, out of nowhere, Maverick trips over a rock and has fallen into yet another big pile of mud.

"SPLASH"

"Oh no," he tells them "It's always me isn't it," he says wiping his now muddy face on the back of his sleeve.

Conor helps him back up and smiles at the state of him

"You know Maverick, You've got a little bit of mud, there," he says

"Where?" Maverick asks as he points at his face frantically trying to wipe it again

"No, It's just there," he says pointing all over his body and jabbing him in the ribs, which makes them both laugh. They then continue to smile as they both carry on forward following the other two further down into Pickle Lane.

Suddenly they notice a dark figure that's standing at the entrance of Pickle Lane, shouting at them, from where they've just walked through around three minutes ago, his shouts startle our heroes and they can't really make out what he's shouting at them.

"Stop a minute, what's he saying?" Conor says looking back towards the figure

"Come back here" they hear him shout, "Come back here now!!" It's a man's voice, one they don't really recognise "You need to come back, you don't know what you're doing, it's a trap" he shouts again "You need to come back now, you're going to be in danger,"

This causes our heroes to break into a run and when they finally reach the end of Pickle lane, they look back and the figure that was behind them has now disappeared… Now…to mention it…. it looks as if the whole street has disappeared along with Pickle Lane but our heroes don't seem to be too worried, as they are met with the warm, glorious sun shining high in the sky as well as the large bunch of multicoloured balloons.

"Look at these labels," Lucas says

As he picks up one of the labels attached to one of the balloons, he can't help but notice each one has a funny-looking sign on it

"They're so cool, but I wonder what that sign is," he asks

And on closer inspection, they all notice it too.

"I know what that is," Conor says

"Oh you would," Maverick jokes and this makes Conor laugh

"No, honestly I do"

They all stand there silent for a few moments waiting for Conor to tell them.

"So??" Rosienna says as they wait on Conor

"Oh sorry…. I just….haven't seen that sign for a while"

"Where have you seen it?" Lucas asks

"Nana….she showed it to be once or twice….she said that it means Endless love and Connection I think"

"What does that even mean?" Maverick asks him

"You know what, I'm not sure she just said it was like an endless thing"

"But why would it be attached to these balloons?" Rosienna asks

"I'm not sure," Conor says

"Hang on a minute turn that label over, I saw something," Lucas says

And it reads "You must only take two"

"But why only two?" Maverick asks and you can hear the disappointment in his voice.

"I'm not sure, but there must be a reason," Conor says

They all look at each other and do as the label asks, they each take two balloons and continue on the walk forward through what seems to be at first an extremely large, green forest, with the most magnificent tall trees, wildlife running wildly, the most stunning streams and waterfalls, as well as bushes of all colours, a fresh smell fills there noses and its rather calming, they are definitely surrounded by the most beautiful scenery, but as they continue forward down what seemed to be a windy path covered in what seems to be pebbles ….I would say around ten more feet….. they watch as the forest slowly disappears around them…. and to their surprise, they realise that the ground beneath their feet has now turned into soft golden sand, and all the greenery has once again disappeared and it has been replaced with the highest mountains and it's almost as if they are surrounded by a desert.

"Look!!!" Maverick says excitedly "Now we can build sandcastles," he bends down and starts building a small mound

"Come on Maverick, we need to follow this road, not make sand castles," Rosienna tells him and he gets back up on his feet and follows the rest of them, you can tell he's a little annoyed because all he wants to do is play in the sand surrounding him.

Our heroes walk for a short while longer, when they come across a large tent just off the side of the road, it looks as though it was once white in colour but is now a light brown, kind of beige colour, with the same infinity sign on the side….not that our heroes have even noticed this. This tent is almost like the one you would find an old Indian chief sitting inside beside a small fire pit and chanting sounds, wearing a large feather hat. They all pause outside and it's almost as though they're waiting for each other to go in first.

"Let's go in," Conor tells them in an excited tone

"I'm …. I'm not sure it's safe," Lucas replies

"I'm with Lucas on this one," Rosienna says "What if there's something in there?"

"You're not SCARED are you," Maverick teases them

"No we are not" Rosienna replies "Are we, Lucas?"

"Nooo," he tells them as he starts to feel nervous and is unable to control the quiver in his voice

"Well you two can go first then," Maverick tells them

"Fine" Rosienna replies in a cross tone and a scowl has appeared across her face, as she takes Lucas's hand and drags him inside the tent with her against his will.

Chapter Two
The Tent

Rosienna stands there looking around the tent and she is utterly surprised and thrilled by what they have both found. To their surprise, there isn't an Indian chief in sight at all, no fire burning in a fire pit and no one singing songs, but in front of them is the most pleasant, comfortable, and cosy-looking room.

"Wow, I didn't think it would be like this," Rosienna says "It's huge, way bigger than it looks from the outside…. I never want to leave!!"

"This is so cool…. if I could build a room, I would definitely do it like this one," Lucas says "You guys have got to see this" he shouts to the other two and it's not long before they're joined by Maverick and Conor.

They all stand there all agog and you can tell that the excitement has started to fill them, when they look around the room they notice that it seems bigger than it looked on the outside and that it's almost the size of nine or ten cars put together, They first notice that there are hundreds of beautiful white fairy lights, twinkling as they hang all around the tent walls, as well as multi-coloured bunting hanging from the centre of the roof branching outwards to the tent walls too, there's a funny looking wardrobe thing to the right of the room and to the left is a large wooden trunk, as well as a huge wooden table that's completely covered in food…. You know…. the nice things like…. pasties, sausage rolls, chicken, mini sandwiches, burgers, fries, crisps, pineapple and cheese, cookies, cakes of all flavours, fruits from all over the world, ice cream, lots of different sweets, all different biscuits and lots of fizzy pop and fruit juice.

All over the tent floor, there are huge, padded, multi-coloured rugs made from the finest materials and something that surprises them but thrills them at the same time is that half of the tent is completely full of the softest cushions that you've ever felt, cushions of all materials and colours…. Blue and purple cotton, black silk, soft yellow and orange ones, red velvet, pink satin, and green silk.

Maverick is the first to take a dive into all the cushions and he very quickly starts to disappear within them, after only a few moments he has completely disappeared within them and there's no sign of him.

"Maverick?" Conor says as he can no longer see him

"Maverick" Rosienna says mirroring his words

"Maverick" Conor says again his voice suddenly full of panic

"Stop messing around," Rosienna says as she now starts to feel quite cross with him

"Maverick where are you?" Lucas says as he also starts to panic because it's been a few minutes now and there's still no sign of him.

They all look at each other before running forward, picking up the cushions and throwing them behind them, trying to find where he's disappeared to, hoping they can dig him out, but these cushions are deep and there are hundreds of them.

He finally reappears in the middle of the room grinning and laughing at them all, Conor rolls his eyes but looks relieved, Lucas laughs, and Rosienna looks cross but they can't help but smile back at him with a look of relief on her face.

"Don't do that again…. You scared us," she says "there could be anything down there," Rosienna says

"You've got to try this," he tells the others, his voice full of excitement and pride "It's so much fun"

"Maverick that's not funny," Rosienna tells him in a cross tone, "We thought you had disappeared"

"Don't be silly no one can just disappear…. I'm not magic,"

After a lot of running around and several plates of food later, They all find the softest blankets that were hidden within the wooden wardrobe along with some other things… they then all sit down and get comfortable on the super-soft cushions.

Rosienna lies down on her side covering herself in her warm pink spotted blanket, including her head, and Lucas decides to do the same with his orange velvet one, for some reason his blanket feels heavy, Maverick buries himself within the cushions again so only his face is visible once more, but he's decided to cuddle his baby blue blanket as he says it smells just like Nana Sharon….but that must be nonsense because …..it can't….. can it?.... and Conor lays flat on his back with a grey lightweight blanket over the top of him, facing the tent roof so that if he needs to he can still look around the room at the others – he's always been the one who looks out for them all.

"Oh my…I'm so tiiiireddd" Rosienna says with a stretch and a yawn

"Me too…My eyes feel all funny" says Maverick as he rubs them and is struggling to keep them open

"I'm so full, I think I might have eaten too much," Lucas tells his friends with a big stretch and yawn too "I'm full right up to my neck,"

And you can hear Maverick giggle at these words because who can be full up to their neck?

"Maybe we could just lay here and rest our eyes for a few minutes," Conor also tells them with a yawn

And it's as if it's catching, before they know it our hero's eyes have become heavy and they have all fallen into a deep sleep.

Chapter Three
The Floof

Lucas is the first to wake a short while later, he rubs his eyes, stretches out, and then sits up. He feels hot, and gosh…. it's warm in this tent…. and he looks around to see where his friends are, he can see that there all snuggled uptight and still fast asleep.

Maverick's gentle snores fill the tent and Conor turns over onto his left side as Rosienna lies catching flies. It's still light outside, did the night even come?......

Lucas can see the sun shining through the tent walls, he wonders how long they've all been asleep and suddenly out of nowhere he spots a small ball of grey fluff beside his feet, he sits and looks at it curiously for a moment and briefly wonders if it's a very round, very fluffy cushion but there are no others like it in here, what could it be? He wonders, and how has it even found its way in here,? it feels warm against his feet but as he moves forward to look a little closer, he decides he wants to run his hands over it to see how soft it is, when suddenly its furry face turns round and he can see a pair of big beautiful brown eyes looking straight at him.

"Ahhhhhh," he shouts jumping up and away from the creature, running around to the other side of the tent and frantically waking the others.

"Ahhhhhh," Maverick, Conor, and Rosienna also shout, copying Lucas's screams as they are all so dazed from their sleep and now feeling slightly scared, but not because they are actually scared but because Lucas has shouted and awoken them from their dreams.

The creature lifts its head and it looks just as surprised to see them standing there looking at them as our heroes are to see the creature in the tent.

Rosienna who is a big animal lover, slowly and carefully walks towards the creature, she bends down and kneels beside it, almost afraid to touch it.

"Don't get too close," Conor tells her as he watches her stretch out her hand towards it. "It might be dangerous"

"Hey little buddy it's okay," she says "Don't be scared…we won't hurt you"

She reaches her hand down to touch it and it lifts its head straight into the palm of her hand, almost as if it's telling her it's okay I'm not scared of you, Rosienna smiles at the creature and this encourages the others to come just a little closer but just not as close as her, they're still a little worried about who and what this creature is or might be.

After a short time, curiosity gets the better of them and now the boys all scoot a little closer so that all our heroes are now sitting around the mound of hair just like Rosienna, who has begun to stroke it and it rolls around amongst all the cushions making our heroes smile.

"I wonder if you have a name," Rosienna says out loud as she looks for a collar around its neck, she finds one but there seems to be no name tag and it seems to be made of some sort of strange grey and blue plastic material with the infinity sign carved all around it, but the collar itself almost feels like rubber.

"Hey….I do has a name," a funny voice suddenly says

They all look around the tent to see where the voice has come from, but there's no one else in the tent but them and this fluffy funny creature.

"Hey… it's me…. downs heres on the colourful squishes," the voice tells them

"Ahhhh" they all shout as they all realise that the creature has spoken, this causes our heroes to move back away from the creature once again, all apart from Rosienna who is still in front of it wearing an excited grin.

"No, I is not call Ahhhh," it says looking at each of them and this makes them laugh "People has called me a few things in my times….umm… lets me thinks of some's a minutes……umm wells,….yes ….some peoples has called me's "Pup" others has called me "Miss Rosie" and "getaways dog" some peoples just call me "Rose" and sometimes on the odd occasions I has been called floof"

"Ooo hang on you mean Rosie almost like my name?" Rosienna asks

"Yes umm, I thinks,….I means…hang on a minutes… I …umm….I's….do nots thinks I knows your names…. but I has also been called a few more things likes "Do yous wants a treats", "Gods yous stinks" "No, no, no", "Muppet", "Get down" and "for the love of God, Please stops licking your bottoms" so takes your picks I's can answers to whatevers you's likes,"

Our heroes try to hold in their laughter at the word bottom, Obviously, this creature does not know what a bottom is.

"My favourites has to be "Muppet" and "Gods yous stinks" but you may calls me whatever's you wishes"

Our heroes all look at each other and laugh again

"You know those aren't real names don't you?" Lucas tells her with a giggle

"No, they's definitely are's…I has been called them many times"

Lucas looks at the others and smiles a wide tooth grin at her response "Umm…I think we'll just call you Rosie" he tells her

"And you know what?.... I tink's….I tink's I like's it," Rosie replies

They all slowly walk back towards Rosie and sit down around her on the comfortable cushions making sure that there beside one another, they continue to look at each other and this creature, as if they're trying to figure out if this creature who actually looks more like a fluffy dog, really just spoke to them and how she got here in the tent in the first place.

Rosie is a small dog and is grey, white, and brown in fluffy patches of fur, she has the most beautiful brown eyes. Rosie sits looking back at them as if trying to figure out what our heroes are thinking. For a short while, nobody actually says anything, it's Rosienna that chooses to break the silence first as curiosity gets the better of her.

"Rosie …..I….I don't mean to…umm… sound rude or anything but…but …What er… what are you?" she asks

"Umm….wells I can be whatevers I likes but I prefers this forms,"

"You mean a dog?" Maverick asks

"Yes it is much funs to be a dog, I's can runs real fast and eat nice meaty foods, I can jumps high and chase balls all days and not feels tireds, peoples like me because I'm all snugglys and soft and I dare say rather cutes. At the ends of a long days, I can cuddle up in here in these cushions.

"But don't you have any friends?" Lucas asks looking sad for her

"Oh…..I has lots of friends….just in all different places," Rosie tells them "But I's have lots of impert….Import

"You mean Important" Lucas corrects her

"Ahhh…Yes, thanks yous…Important jobs to do's, so I's can be's whatever I wants to be's"

Silence fills the room and they all stand looking at her unsure of what to say, when Conor breaks the silence as he looks at her sceptically

"So if we said a monkey?"

And right before their eye's as if like magic, she somehow changes into a small brown and white squirrel monkey that jumps over to him and climbs up his arm to sit on Conor's right shoulder, she then picks through his hair looking for bugs as only a monkey would.

"Wow," Rosienna says

"That's amazing," Lucas tells her absolutely gobsmacked

"Hang on…. And if we say a cute bunny rabbit?" Rosienna asks excitedly

Once again they all watch as the monkey jumps back down onto the colourful cushions in front of them and transforms into a small fluffy white bunny rabbit, who's now looking at the four of them wiggling its nose and they all smile at her.

"Ooo I know, I know, What about a chicken?" Maverick asks excitedly as he jumps up from the yellow cushion he was just sitting on and he stands so he's right in front of Rosie.

And just like that our fluffy bunny is transformed into a brown and orange chicken that clucks and is now running wildly around the tent, as fast as it can on its two legs, as it tries not to fall over the soft cushions, which makes our heroes laugh.

When she's finished her wild outburst she stops and waddles back towards the children, she then chooses to walk and stand in front of Lucas, looking at him and he looks down at the chicken smiling.

"And yous??" she asks

"Well… I'd really like to see a dragon," Lucas tells her
"But that has to be impossible…Dragons aren't real"

"Ohhh aren't theys? …nothings is impossibles if yous
wants it enough….now close your eyes," says the
chicken

They all do as she asks but they can feel something
getting very big and suddenly they open their eyes to
find that the chicken that was in front of them has
disappeared and reappeared as an orange dragon that
is flying around the tent before landing heavily in
front of them. Which is met with a lot of "Ooo's,
ahhh's and a couple of wow's" when she lands in the
tent it shakes slightly and they watch as the dragon
quickly transforms back into a small fluffy grey dog.

"Sees I can bees whatever you wants me's to
bees….and you's can be's whatever you want to too,"
she tells them aloud "you's knows within reasons,"
she says under her breath.

"But we can't do that…" Maverick tells Rosie "and
that was so cool"

"No but you can still be's whoever you want's to be,
you's don'ts has to change for no one and the bigger
you dreams the bigger you can be's"

They all smile at her, Rosienna bends down and
moves closer to scratch behind Rosie's left ear and she
groans in delight.

"Ohhh It's been so longs since someones has done that's…." She groans again and her back leg starts to shake, Rosie stands up and shakes it out and then sits looking up at the four of them.

"What's you's lot called then?" she finally says looking at each of them.

"Well my name is Rosienna," she says as she sits back to look at Rosie "You know kind of like your name,"

"I'm Lucas," he says as he puts a hand up in a little wave

"My names Conor," he says holding out his hand and shaking Rosie's right paw

"Maverick," Maverick tells her with a shy cheeky smile

"Ahhh….And what's a nice bunch yous are's" she tells them as she then starts to scratch behind her ear "Ohhh sorrwy but I cans not reach it, its has been such a long times since I has been scratched"

"Shall I help you, Rosie?" Lucas asks her as he leans forward and scratches the back of her neck.

"Ahhh…that's….ooo….that is much betters, thanks you young Sirs," she says as she sinks down onto the cushions she sitting on and it's as if you can just watch her relax in front of them.

"Your welcome Rosie," he replies

"So tells mes, how did yous all's get heres in the realm of times"

"We're....We're...Umm... not entirely sure" Conor says glumly

"Well, do tells me's something.... Do yous all's likes an adventure?"

Chapter Four

A Quest

"Wₑ all love an adventure…don't we," Maverick

says as he looks around at his friends

"Yes definitely," Lucas says enthusiastically

"Of course we do," Rosienna tells her with a smile

"Sometimes, as long as there's fun to be had," Conor
tells Rosie

"Well, I do's believes that there is always funs to be
has on this adventure,"

They all look at her and can't help but feel rather confused and then at each other and you can spot the look of worry on Lucas's face.

"There is no needs to worries, The ones that they calls Lucas, yous is perfectly safes withs me's"

Lucas gives her a weak smile and you can tell he's trying to figure out if he can trust and believe her. Rosienna notices this and takes his hand once more, she has always been the one to give him courage and to make him feel brave.

But the question is, is can our heroes really trust Rosie?……

"Comes withs mes," Rosie says as she walks them over to the left side of the tent "Tell's me what's do you's knows about time?"

They all stand there looking around at one another, a look of confusion across their faces

"I don't understand," Rosienna says

"What do's you knows about time?" Rosie asks again

They all stand there looking at Rosie and there are confused faces all around, as silence fills the tent once more

"Hang on a minute….Do you mean as in a clock, kind of like the time?" Lucas asks

"No, not quite,"

"As in history?" Conor asks

"Well, yes buts not's just history and the pasts,"

"We learnt about the world wars last year in my class," Maverick tells her

"That's very good's, but tells me's what's did they teach you's about the future?" Rosie asks

They all look at one another once more feeling rather confused.

"Nothing…Because it hasn't happened yet" Rosienna tells her feeling even more confused.

"Hasn't it's?" Rosie says questioningly "Let's me ask's you's this, if yous four could's travel in times where woulds yous choose to goes?....just yous have a seat on those cushions right there's and think about it for a fews minutes"

And our heroes do as they're told, they each sit down on the cushions, - Lucas on a Blue, Conor on a Black silk one, Rosienna on a purple, and Maverick on a green - they sit for a while thinking hard about what Rosie had just asked them. While she sits patiently watching them. When finally Lucas goes to speak but she stops him.

"Ahhh no's, no's don't tells us….It's would be much betters if you's shows us?" Rosie tells them

Lucas looks at Rosie and he just seems so confused by her request – it's as if she's not making much sense at all.

"But Rosie…. I'm not sure that we understand….what do you mean? How can we show you?" Rosienna asks her

And silence fills the tent once more.

"Will's you's all helps me a moments please?"

Rosie's now met with, "Okay's, a sure" and a few nods from our heroes, they all get to their feet and follow Rosie to the very edge of the tent.

"Rosienna, if yous could's just lift that green cushion just there's, Lucas if yous could lift that orange ones, and Maverick could yous lift that blue ones just there's please?"

"This one?" Rosienna asks pointing in the direction of the cushions in front of her

"Please," Rosie says

They all do as Rosie has asked them, and what she reveals are three small odd-looking wooden boxes, each box is different and has a small clasp on each of them at the front, and the infinity sign on the front of each box.

Rosie sits looking at our heroes before saying "Each of these boxes contains threes things for each of you's, all three things will be useful to yous on your adventures,"

"They look like small treasure chests," Maverick tells them

"Yeah, they do" Lucas agrees

"Excuse me Rosie but…umm what do you mean our adventure?" Conor asks now curious

"The adventures you's is going on…don't worry you'll know when's yous gets there," she tells them "Now Miss Rosienna, could yous open that first box please?"

Chapter Five
The Boxes

Rosienna does as she's asked and bends down to the first wooden box, the others scoot closer to get a better look as they lean in closer, The box (that does indeed look like a small treasure chest) is covered in the most beautiful blue and white diamonds. Rosienna carefully lifts the lid and hidden inside you can see what looks like four, glowing blue, watch-like devices, Similar to the one that's around Rosie's neck forming her collar.

"Oh wow," we hear Conor say

"Hang on. are we going to be dogs?" Maverick asks and the others shoot him a look as if to say don't be so silly "What?...we could be"

"What are they?" Conor asks

"That's is a very goods questions the ones they's calls Conor," Rosie tells them and he looks at her with a slightly worried expression on his face.

"Please takes ones each" she continues

"They're so cool," Lucas says as he bends down to take one from the treasure box

"But doesn't it match what's on your collar?"

"You is correct, Rosienna" and she bends down to take one too and Maverick and Conor do the same

"They don't really look like watches, there's no hands or any digital time on them….are they broken?" Maverick asks

"No, that's how they's supposed to be's," Rosie tells them.

"But what are they for?" Lucas asks

"Your wrists," Rosie tells them "They is likes the bracelet things you humans sometimes wear"

Rosie watches as they all place the devices on their wrists, at first they all seem to look pretty as they start to glow blue and our heroes are all smiling

"Wow….these are so cool," Lucas says

"I know I love how they glow," Conor tells them
"Can we keep them?" Conor asks

"I can't believe we're all glowing....look," Rosienna says as she holds her wrist out in front of her, "These are amaz……"

And suddenly Rosienna stops talking, and the bracelets start to tighten around their wrists, and we watch as our heroes all start to panic and freak out.

"What's happening?" Rosienna asks

"Ahhh it's stuck," Maverick says

"Rosie, what do we do?" Conor asks

Our heroes frantically try to pull them back off their wrists

"It's stuck, it's stuck on my wrist," Lucas says

"Mine too," says Maverick

"Rosie, what's going on?" Conor asks

"Aww yes, maybe I shoulds has mentioned that's…There is no needs to be scared children, they are for your safety and will allow me to help yous and take off on your adventures" Rosie tells them in a calm tone, "they wills nots hurts yous I do promise"

You can see our heroes taking in her words and starting to calm down.

"Lucas, if you woulds…could's you now opens the next box please?"

Once again Lucas walks over to the next box and notices this box is covered in green and emerald diamonds, he does as he's told and carefully lifts the lid. Inside he finds four white feathers all neatly laid out on a green velvet padded cushion and tucked neatly down the back of the box, he finds a very old, very tarnished looking letter in an envelope, which has been sealed by a red wax and is stamped with a what looks like a clock face, we watch as he very gently peels back the envelope and starts to read:

Hello Children,

I have been waiting to meet you for a very long time and if you are reading this now you must be in the realm of time, and you would have already been asked to open the first and second boxes, to discover their secrets. The first box is known as the box of the Time Keeper, Which would contain four of the best and rarest, enchanted watches, these are for the use of time travel and will take you where ever you wish to go.

You can go to anytime in the past or present or anytime in the future, You can go back to when dinosaurs ruled the earth, you could go forward to see what life is like in the future or you could simply go back to only a few months ago, the decision is entirely yours individually, but remember to choose wisely.

Rosie will show you how to use them as she has the knowledge of this due to her wearing one for a long period of time, you may have noticed this as her collar. please do not be alarmed they will light up along with Rosie's collar when you use them and have decided where you are headed.

Please be warned, you may face some tricky challenges ahead, challenges that can be extremely dangerous or that could seriously impact other people and their everyday lives, So please be careful to make the best and wisest choices not only for yourself but for others around you too, things that you do in time could affect how your life is today.

However, there are some ground rules I need to make you aware of and that you must follow -

1. *You must always travel together*

2. *You must never tell anyone what year/ time you're from*

3. *Rosie is to go everywhere with you all at all times – she is your*

guide and will always keep you safe.

4. Make sure you are wary of all the people around you they may not be as nice as they seem.

5.   You'll need to work as a team at all times

6. And Nobody is to get left behind

You will have also just opened the box of thought, this is a very helpful tool for you to use, and all you have to do is think about an object and it will appear in front of you, ready to use.

For this to work you must take the white feather from within this box and hold it tight in your hands, closing your eyes and thinking hard about the object that you wish to receive, this may be something that you may simply find useful to you on your adventure. It is very easy to use and I'm sure you'll get the hang of it.

In your last and final box, you will find the bag of the healer and one of the five Pocket watches, all created and given by the Violet witch. This is a small pocket bag that may seem very small but I can assure you that inside it is rather large, but its size is handy and can fit inside one of your smallest pockets, you can keep all of the things we have given you inside.

The Pocket watch from the Violet witch, is the most important thing of all, keep it safe and never let it out of your sight, there will be people on your journey, people that aren't always nice, who will try and take the Pocket watches from you. There will be four more for you to collect throughout time but it won't be easy, you must know that each watch contains a special key, Rosie can show you this when you have all five.

Oh and one more thing, the balloons that you would have found on your way in here, you should have each taken only two. When they burst they will bring you back to this very tent, now some may burst accidentally but you need to make sure that you have at least one each to enable you all to come home from your worlds.

God bless and good luck on your adventure, hopefully, I'll see you all soon, Stay safe and Lucas remember to be brave.

Regards

V. Monty

The children become very excited by this letter, as it explains a little about what's about to happen, what's in the boxes, and what's expected of our heroes, But they have so many questions that they are all bursting to ask Rosie.

"Why is the pocket watch so special?" Lucas asks

"Who is V . Monty?" Conor asks

"Where are we going?" Maverick asks

"Who wants the pocket watches?" Rosienna asks

Rosie looks at them all in front of her and finally says "Shhh" to try and get them to calm down and be quiet "Please do not worry small heroes, I know you do's has a lot's of questions nows and I cans certainly answer them for yous, but please ones at a times, we have plenty's of times,"

"Where are we going?" Maverick asks again

"Like the letters mentions, where ever yous wishes to goes, but yous must remembers to all choose wiselys"

"Why do some many people want the pocket watches?" Lucas asks

"Ahhh, now that's is a good questions, the pockets watch is not the thing that peoples want, it is whats lies withins them that they requires, it was once given by the Violet witch to a young girl around fifty years ago, it has the ability to change times completely and bring back things that once weres, yous could's say it unlocks treasures "

They all look at Rosie with a concerned but excited look

"It also can changes the courses of times and we believes that it is essential that they's is destroyed, in the wrong hands it could's be used for no good, howevers, what is in the pockets watches is extremely useful's to us"

"But who wants the pocket watches so much?" Rosienna asks

"I would say that's kind of obvious" Maverick tells her and she scowls at him.

"Well, there's is only a fews that knows about thems"

"I wouldn't say it's obvious," Rosienna tells him

"It's the bad guys," Maverick tells her and she shoots him a look as if to say I know that.

"But Rosie, what's in the watch?" Conor asks as he buts in

"Something's we needs, we shalls opens them togethers, and yous shall see's"

They all look at one another as if unsure of what is about to happen next, but you can see how the excitement is starting to fill them and there are smiles all around, Lucas can't seem to keep still, while Rosienna bounces up and down on the balls of her feet wearing her biggest smile, Maverick just stands there and is all smiles but is becoming all giggly but he does seem to be rather nervous, Conor is very serious and takes a confident step closer to Rosie.

"Lucas where's are we goings? I needs yous to type a date of your choice into your watch," Rosie tells him

He looks down at his wrist and notices that the watch-like device has lit up blue just like he notices Rosie's collar has done the same, they all stand there looking at their watches, then to back to him as he puts in some numbers and then they all hear a beeping noise.

"Ready? Nows holds hands and let's go on an adventure,"

Lucas's Adventure

Chapter Six

The First Adventure

The next thing our heroes know is that they are being flown through what seems to be a long black tunnel with multicoloured stars dotted all around them, it's as if the stars are moving extremely fast and whizzing past them, or maybe our heroes are shooting stars themselves….I'm not sure.

"Woah…this is amazing," Lucas says and he can hear the giggles of his friends from around him

Rosienna starts to giggle louder

"It's just like being on a rollercoaster or in a spaceship" she yells to the others "This is the best moment of my life!!!" she continues as she looks back around at Conor who's also wearing the biggest smile and Maverick who's now matching her giggle.

After a short while, things seem to be slowing down but as our heroes look around them, they can see that the colourful stars have seemed to have settled all around them and have slowed down to the point where it's almost as if they're gently floating among them.

The next thing our heroes know is everything has gone dark, the stars have now started to disappear around them and after a few minutes, they can no longer see them as they are plunged into darkness, looking down at their wrists they can see that the lights on their watches have gone out too, and they have absolutely no idea where they are.

"Oh god," Rosienna says

"Where are we?" Conor asks as he taps on his watch trying to figure out what just happened

"Lucas where did you take us?" Maverick asks him

"I...I....I don't know, we're supposed to be where there are lots of lights and fun things to do"

Conor puts his hands out in front of him, trying to feel where they all are when he finally touches something that feels like the tent walls.

"I think we're still inside the tent," he tells them as he feels around some more "…..never mind, I think that was just a coat"

He turns slightly right and walks forward some more

"Oh, God where are we?" we hear Maverick say

When you hear a sudden bang which kind of sounds like one of them has fallen into a drum kit or something that makes that sound.

"OUCH" we hear a voice say that we recognise to be Lucas's

"Are you okay?" Rosienna asks

"Yeah…. I think so…I think I just fell over some saucepans"

"Try putting your hands out in front of you" they hear Conor's voice say, "I think I've found the tent walls"

They do as he's suggested, our heroes all put their arms out in front of themselves and they too can feel the tent walls and it's as though they're still in the tent that they were in just moments ago.

"Hang on were still in the tent" we hear Lucas's voice say

"Didn't it work?" Rosienna asks

"I'm not sure," Maverick says

"Of course, its has worked" a voice they now recognise to be Rosie's says – which is reassuring as our heroes were just beginning to wonder if Rosie was real or not.

"Over here " Conor calls

Suddenly there's a small slither of light as he folds back the side of the tent to reveal the most wonderful scene that's unfolding in front of our heroes, they quickly realise that they weren't in the tent that they were in only a few moments ago.

First, our heroes look back, looking up at the tent they were just standing in and they notice that it's covered in blue and green stripes, with a small white flag flying from the top.

They all stand looking out at the scene before them as it unfolds in front of their eyes and what they see before is something rarely seen back at home.

"Yes, we're here!!!," Lucas says as the excitement fills him and he jumps up and down, they all look around all agog smiling at one another.

"This place is amazing" Lucas, says "Much better than I ever imagined"

"Wow, look at that" Rosienna says as she points in the direction of the huge, beautiful, merry-go-round, that is playing the most beautiful song. The horses are all brown, white and black and all so delicately decorated, all with a gold outline around their names which sit elegantly on the side of their necks, with a freshly painted brown seat and as our heroes stand watching, you can notice the fine details on these horses are just so magnificent, that they almost look real from a short distance, our heroes stand and watch admiring them as they go up and down with the music, we can spot so many smiling faces sitting upon them – I mean why would you be sad sat upon that ride.

"I definitely would like to go on that," Rosienna says as our heroes leave the tent and walk further towards it "I love how pretty those horses are!!"

"Oh look they all have names!" Lucas says as they get closer.

The fairground is just glorious, everything looks so new but old at the same time, each ride is delicately hand painted in greens, blues, yellows, reds and pinks, but these colours do look a little dull but there are gold outlines around the rides and letters delicately painted on all of them, its different to see that most of the rides have been hand made out of wood unlike the metal and plastic ones that they have back at home, there are also lights dotted around the fairground which are made up of red, yellow, pink, and blue lights which twinkle to the soothing music.

As our heroes walk a little further into the fairground they notice that they are surrounded by a sea of people, and it's magnificent to see that there isn't a grumpy or a sad face in sight everyone seems so happy and grateful to be there.

"I would like to go on the rockets to the moon," Maverick says as he points out a ride in the distance, which is a ride that has different coloured and numbered rockets attached to it. This ride only holds two people at one time and the rockets whiz around really fast, but instead of the ride going around in circles, it goes around up towards the sky and back down again, we watch as you can see people laughing and having the best time – this ride is supposed to give the riders the idea that this would be what it would feel if you should ever get the chance to go to the moon.

Our heroes pass many rides as they walk through the fairground, taking in all its wonderful sights, I mean it's not every day you get to visit a vintage fairground. The rides include some that our heroes have never seen before, rides like the "Helter-Skelter" – which is kind of like a cone shape ride with white and red stripes all around it with a big twisty slide around the outside of the cone, "The Merri-go-round" dances in circles in all its glory, the horses gracefully dancing up and down as the beautiful music plays, as they walk a little further they come across "The Waltsers" – which is a ride that whizzes around fast, the beige and gold carts are spinning too while the rider sits upon red velvet cushions and if the attendants don't think your going fast enough, they'll come and spin you faster, "a flying car" ride where people are laughing and curiously enjoying the ride – because who new cars could fly in 1925, as well as a motorbike ride called "Speed" – where riders sit on wooden motor cycles and hold on for dear life as they spin around at high speed, we watch as the riders are holding on tightly but laughing, there's also a ride that you don't see very often and that's a ride where people sit within what seems to be "Hot Air Balloons" and it moves them up and down. As they walk a little further Lucas spots his favourite ride of all, "The Dodgems" which have all different coloured carts or cars whichever you'd like to call them and are driving around and there are people once again all smiling if not laughing…. All apart from one lady who seems to be holding on to her hat on her head rather tightly and the side of the yellow cart as her male companion drives.

They walk a short distance more and that's when our heroes….well they hear it before they see it, a huge stage with three of the most beautiful ladies in frilly white dresses that are sitting upon swings which are covered in flowers, singing at the top of their lungs, along with an organ that's playing beautifully behind them, they look to their right and see a huge, big white ride known as the "Big Wheel" and the queue looks huge.

"I bet you can see everything from up there," Conor says

They walk a little further and can't help but spot "The Ghost Train" which looks surprisingly, the least scary thing you have ever seen. As they continue to walk further forward they can't help but notice the very large tent in the middle of the fairground.

"What is that?" Rosienna asks

"I think, it might be a circus tent" Lucas, tells her looking at the blue and white striped tent with two large white flags

"I woulds say's that's definitely a circus tents," Rosie says "I bet there is some funs to be has in there's"

"Can we go in there, Rosie?" Maverick asks

"Yes I thinks that would be's a fun thing to do's"

Chapter Seven

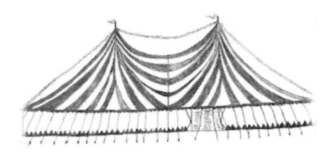

The Circus

W e find our heroes making their way towards
the big top tent, they get their tickets from the small
red and yellow booth just outside, (which seems to be
made from yellow cardboard that has red edging to
them) after figuring out how to use their white
feathers, so that money appeared in front of them
enabling them to get in. They then enter the tent and
make their way towards the wooden benches to take a
seat with Rosie sitting between them, Luckily they
manage to find seats on the second row from the
front. A man who introduces himself as the
ringmaster enters the large ring which is in the centre
of the tent

"Good Afternoon, Ladies and Gentlemen, Boys and
Girls….Welllllcome to Thurston's terrific Circus!!!…."

and there's a round of applause from the crowd "We have travelled far and wide to be here with you here today Ladies, gentlemen, boys and girls" his voice booms "and haven't we got some real treats here for you ....and maybe even some surprises here for you tonight.....So sit tight, and let us first welcome our very first act,....Talia and Thomas our trapeze artists......"

The crowd around them claps and they watch as darkness falls all around them, a large light shines high above them onto a woman casually swinging on what seems to be a long swing, she swings elegantly when suddenly she turns herself upside down so that she's hanging from her legs casually swinging backwards and forwards. You can hear the shocked sounds from the crowd when suddenly a man jumps out to grab her hands, they both swing backwards and forwards, elegantly doing tricks in the air above our heroes. A few minutes later they see Acrobats, jugglers and Fire performers and there seems to be a certain buzz of amazement within the tent.

"How do they do that and not get burnt?" Maverick asks

"I don't know" Lucas, says "but I definitely want to try it"

"I can't believe that they've managed to catch all those juggling balls," Rosienna says to them.

They then watch as elephants are brought out with performers riding upon their backs all together there are four of them including what looks like a baby elephant holding on to the tail of one of the larger ones, they're wearing the most exquisite beaded headdresses. Our heroes watch as the elephants balance up against each other and up on platforms, and as they end the act the two performers get lifted up so that they are sitting upon the elephant's trunks.

"Whoa," Rosienna says "I want to be able to do that"

Once the elephants leave the ring, the clowns ascend, they madly run around spraying people with water from the flowers that are either in their hands or the ones that are pinned to their tops, they run around falling into one another and tipping over almost nothing, we watch as another small clown comes out holding a pole with buckets of water at each end, he turns around almost hitting the other clowns as they make out that there trying to help him but when he turns around he hits two of them to the floor and laughter fills the tent.

"They are so funny" Lucas, says laughing

"Yeah they are," Maverick says laughing too

"He knocked them down," Rosienna says pointing and laughing at them.

We next watch as the strong man walks into the centre of the ring, he's wearing what looks like a leopard skin long t-shirt, almost like one you could see a caveman wearing, he has a bold head and he has the longest black moustache you have ever seen. He tries to lift all different sized weights and he manages to lift all three, we watch as two lady performers dressed in beaded gowns enter the ring and sit upon the pole and he manages to lift them too with a smile, and the crowd cheers.

Next, are the type rope performers balancing high above and walking along the rope, first of all, the man balances extremely well and when he gets to the middle of the rope he starts to wobble, but out of nowhere he seems to steady himself and starts doing handstands and jumping upon the wire, he then starts spinning around the rope and then lands back on top of it, soon he's joined by another man that climbs on his shoulders and they balance as they walk from one end of the rope to the other, finally they walk back to the middle, take a bow and their act is over.

The acts go on for the next few hours and our heroes take in the sights with a lot of Ooo's and ahhh's. Of course, the clowns make another few appearances, and there's an act with a small monkey and a dog who's doing tricks, when they have finished suddenly the ringmaster entered the ring once more.

"I WANT YOU TO MEET THE WORLD'S WONDERFUL AND WEIRD FREAKS!" he bellows

He introduces them as they enter the ring but personally, I don't see that there was anything wrong with these people, they just looked rather different.

"MAY I INTRODUCE TO YOU THE ONE....THE ONLY...... MARY THE BEARDED LADY!" he bellows

Who stands there awkwardly and is just a young woman with a beard, to which Rosienna says "I don't understand why this is an act, I could grow a beard if I want to"

"DOG BOY" he bellows again

Who is just a young man who is extremely hairy and we watch as he gets on all fours and moves around the ring like a dog.

"THE IRISH GIANT"

In which we see an extremely tall man enter the centre of the ring too.

"I've never seen anyone so tall in my life! This is so cool" Maverick says

"THE GENERAL....MR TOM THUMB"

He enters the ring upon horseback and was called the smallest man in the world but at his entrance, there are a few gasps and squeals before silence falls upon the ring.

"THE GILLIAN SISTERS PHYLLIS AND GERTRUDE" and we watch as an extremely thin lady and a rather large lady also enter.

"AND LAST BUT NOT LEAST THE SIAMESE TWINS" – that were in fact just twins wearing the same white long shirts and their hair up in tight buns.

"Rosie....I....I don't understand," Rosienna says "how are they freaks....they're just normal people like me and you" she whispers

"Tings, were differents in 1925 Miss Rosienna.....society was not as acceptings as they are back in your times....you daren't bes different to anyone else in 1925"

"But that's not fair," Rosienna says

"But that was the ways of their lives"

"So they kind of became famous for the way they looked?" Lucas asks

"You coulds say's that yes Lucas peoples would comes from far and wide just to see anyone who was not likes thems"

Finally, we watch as the ringmaster walks back into the centre of the ring.

"AND FOR OUR FINAL ACT.....PLEASE WELCOME SINA, STEVEN AND THEIR FURRY FRIENDS MAPLE AND MALCOLM"

As we look at the ring, a beautiful woman and man walk into the ring holding hands and following close behind them are two lions, we watch as they stalk around the ring, and they are just majestic. As we look around the tent you can see a lot of horrified & scared faces.

"I've never seen a lion up close before," Rosienna says

"Me either," Conor, says "There so pretty"

The show finishes with a Raw from the lions and the room falls silent, and you can tell no one is sure what's about to happen next and that there all slightly scared for their lives. Once the lions are ushered back behind the curtains once more it seems that you can see everyone around the ring relax.

"THAT'S ALL FOLKS...BE SURE TO COME BACK AND SEE US AGAIN SOON" the ringmaster says at this everyone stands and makes their way to the entrance of the tent that they came through on their way in, Our heroes also make their way to the exit and back out into the fairground.

As they look to the left of the circus tent and they can't help but notice a few more tents and stalls full of activities, one tent that's red and white striped has a fortune teller sitting with a crystal ball in front of her. The next one they come to has a sign above a stall that reads "The Hall of Mirrors" where there are lots of people smiling and laughing from within it. Just across from there is a ride called "The Love Boat" which is a ride for couples or people who were "courting" – Courting was a word used back then to describe people going out on dates, the little boats float upon a fake river and you can see people kissing as they come out the other side - There's also a rollercoaster called "The Thunderbolt" and a ride called the "Wild Mouse" which is almost like small cars on a rollercoaster track, and a flying chair ride – in which people would be seated and lifted into the air, which was designed to make the rider feel like they were flying, something spectacular that our heroes notice is there are the most detailed steam trains to their left all lined up, in dark green, navy blue and burgundy with a gold line detail around the sides which has been hand-painted on, highlighting its name, in total, we count around eleven of them.

"You don't see these anymore" Lucas, says

"What are they?" Maverick asks

"They're called steam trains, they are powered by coal, but you don't see them back home very often"

"Oh, why not?" Maverick asks

"They're very rare, but I guess this is what they would have looked like new" Conor replies

"But what are they used for?" Rosienna asks

"Well, people use to ride on them to travel to different towns, or pull things along…you know like those carriages over there, that the circus would have travelled in, they never used to have cars like we do back home"

As they walk a little further, Lucas then looks to the other side of the fairground and spots "a Punch and Judy" doing a show with loads of young children sitting beneath it all listening and smiling, the next thing that catches his eye are all the games he hasn't yet had a chance to play.

"Look" Lucas, tells them

As he points at all the games surrounding him - like the hook the duck game, a ball throwing game where you have to hit the coconuts off the stands, the strong man game where you would try and see how hard you can hit the machine and bell at the top with a large rubber hammer and the game where you can see if you can hit people in the face with a wet sponge as they put there faces in cut out holes with painted pictures on a wooden board

"I never want to leave" Lucas continues. "look at all those prizes" he points

But the prizes aren't things like plastic toys like we have in 2023 they're all old and random – you know, wooden toys that have been carved from wood, tin soldiers and metal animals, teddy bears and handmade dolls, as well as chocolate treats, sweets, and candy floss.

"Well, what are we waiting for?" Conor says with a smile and our heroes all go to walk away from one another leaving Rosie sitting behind them.

"Yous wants to explores?" her voice says from behind them

This stops our heroes in their tracks, almost as if they've just remembered Rosie's there with them. Our heroes all turn around and look down at her, it's clear that they almost forgot why they were here in their excitement and you can see the sadness on their faces, they're all expecting Rosie to tell them they can't go and have fun.

"I am's just kidding's," Rosie tells them with a cheeky laugh "You's can explore for a shorts while's, I dids tells yous we was to has fun, but keep an eye out for that pocket watch, you's, of course, may has fun buts please remember our rules....we's must all sticks together's....and there's are lots of peoples here but nots everyone's is our friends"

They all nod in agreement with her, but as they continue to walk they spot lots of food and games stalls, with people shouting,

"WIN A PRIZE EVERY TIME BOYS AND GIRLS!"

And then they see something they've never seen before something called the living picture, which today would be known as someone acting without saying a word. This is all new to our heroes, they're not used to people just moving their hands around and pulling faces without saying a word. Back home they are used to people acting or on tv shows, another thing that catches their eye is that most of the signs above the rides not only light up but they all have the same thing written, which is Charles Thurston.

"Rosie" Lucas asks, "Who's Charles Thurston?"

"He is the owners of the fairgrounds"

"Like the ringmaster?" he asks

"No, more like the peoples who runs and organises the fairgrounds...you could's calls him the heads of the family's"

"Have you seen those signs?" Rosienna points

They all look to where she's pointed and there are signs that say "YOU CAN WIN, REAL PRIZES AND LADIES CAN WIN TOO"

"What does that even mean that ladies can win too?" she asks, "of course, they can," Rosienna says

"Ahh," Rosie says "Well, in this realm of times womens were nots allowed to do certain things"

"But why?" Rosienna asks "I can do just as much as the boys"

"That was just the ways things were's" Rosie explains

And Rosienna seems to be cross at this "Sometimes I can do more than they boys" she says as she continues to walk forward

The next thing our heroes find is the hall of mirrors to their right, they walk in and there are plenty of people in there - couples, families, children, and the elderly enjoying themselves as they stand in front of the mirrors.

Our heroes walk in and make their way around the mirrors, they stop to laugh as they walk past each individual mirror as they watch themselves changing shape as they stand in front of them, they laugh as the mirrors make them look really tall with big heads, really short with a round waist, another that makes them look wavy, one that makes them look wide, one that makes them look like they're sitting in a swirl, one that makes them look like they're tall and thin and one that makes them look like there's two of them.

Conor looks down at Rosie with a look of concern on his face and when he is sure that people are out of earshot he asks, "Rosie why are they all dressed in such funny clothes?"

And he's right all the people around them are dressed in waistcoats or a shirt and braces, top hats and tails jackets or the most beautiful floor-length gowns in all different colours and hats and everything looks rather old but kind of new at the same time, some of them carrying canes and they all look rather posh. That's when he notices that the people around them have started to stare and keep giving them odd looks.

"They's are not's in funny clothes dear Conor's, this is how all people's dressed in the 1925s," she tells him

Our heroes suddenly feel a little out of place in their t-shirts, jeans, hoodies, jumpers, and trainers with Rosienna in her blue frilly knee-length dress.

"Rosie, I kind of feel like people are beginning to stare at us….I can't help but feel that the way we're dressed is a little out of place for 1925"

"Hmmm… you is right Conkers….I am noticing this too's" Rosie tells him "You do's all look a little different, maybe we needs to changes that"

"Rosie….I mean….what should we do?" Conor asks her again as he looks around them once more, we don't look like they do" and you can tell he's starting to worry.

"Conor your right" Rosienna says "People are starting to stare at us"

"We definitely dressed differently to everyone here," Maverick says

"Umm…. I has an idea…. follows me's…. quick throughs here…. comes this way…the four of you's….come quicks nows,"

Chapter Eight
Gone

They all walk out the other side of the hall of mirrors and quickly follow Rosie into yet another tent, this tent is blue and green, and inside is a small wooden wardrobe and a leather trunk.

"Rosienna you'll's finds gowns in there for yous to wears, and gents if yous opens that trunks over there, then yous wills be able's to wear what is in there….. they's should all's fits you's perfectly"

Rosienna walks over to the dark wood wardrobe and opens the doors to reveal a beautiful floor-length lemon dress with a matching hat, they're similar to what they have seen other ladies walking around wearing.

"So, I'll look like the ladies out there," Rosienna asks pointing to the entrance of the tent

"Yes, that's is the idea's," Rosie says, "And that ones is for yous dear," Rosie tells her "Yous can get dressed over there…you know behind that thingy," she says looking at the ornate wooden room divider behind her and Rosienna follows Rosie's instructions and goes in behind it where she's suggested.

The boys soon open the leather trunk and inside are three off-white shirts, three sets of braces, one red, one black, and the last one brown, as well as two jackets, one navy, the other black, and two pairs of beige trousers and one blue, there are also four pairs of freshly polished shoes, three smart black shoes for the boys and one slightly healed pair for Rosienna, as well as a flat cap in which Lucas has decided to wear and a black top hat that Maverick has decided he wants to wear too…even if it is slightly too big for him.

Once dressed they make their way back out to the fairground in their new to them clothes, they all can't help but look around at each other smiling.

"I like your hat Maverick," Rosienna tells him

"You look pretty Rosienna," Conor says

"Thank you" She replies "it's a pretty dress isn't it"

"That's a cool hat, Lucas," Conor smiles

"Thanks, I like it… do you want to try it on?"

"Yes please" Conor replies and Lucas hands him the hat

Conor puts it on his head and smiles before pulling a funny face and handing it back to Lucas.

"Ahh you's all look wonderful, very much like yous is all from 1925's" Rosie smiles at them "Now let's go and have some funs"

The first thing our heroes notice is that there are hundreds of multi-coloured lights and the sun is starting to fade leaving the sky with beautiful pink clouds, all around the fairground they can see people laughing with one another and having the best time.

"Come on," Rosienna tells them "let's go on the merry-go-round first,"

You can see how excited she truly is, Rosienna chooses her horse on the outside row, which is called Daisy who has a white mane and tail, and has been painted all white too, with gold bits all around the reins and brown seats. The boys sit beside and around her, they each also choose a horse too, Maverick chooses one behind her which is called Trevor, who has white hair and a brown body with lighter spots on its bottom, Lucas sits in front of her and chooses a brown-haired horse called Collin, that's also browned bodied, and it too has gold and blue bits of paint on the seat and reins and Conor chooses to sit beside her on a black-haired and white-bodied horse, who's name is Jack, while Rosie sits in between Conor and Rosienna.

Our heroes all beam with pride as the ride starts to move and there are certainly smiles all around - no really there really are smiles all around, our heroes have hundreds of faces all smiling back at them, as the horses all slowly move up and down, People are stood around the merry-go-round, strangers….. men, women, and children of all ages from 1925, all now wearing similar clothes to them and giving our heroes all a friendly smile, it also seems that the queue has gotten longer than it was, as people wait patiently for their turn.

Once the ride has come to a complete stop our heroes jump down and head towards the ghost train, In which Maverick is extremely excited to sit on, Rosienna sits beside him and Conor behind with Lucas and Rosie sitting on his lap. He takes Lucas's hand as he can see how nervous he's become.

"It won't be that scary Lucas," He tells him "It might not even be scary at all….This is the year 1925's after all"

"I'm not sure about this" Lucas says "It looks kind of scary"

"It'll be okays….promises," Rosie says

The ride starts to move forward and they enter some small double doors and then through into a dark tunnel with bright yellow paint up the walls, they notice a sign that says DANGER in big red writing over-head. The only sound is the sound of the clicking of the train on the track when suddenly an oversized doll drops down in front of them that's clearly hanging from string, which makes them all jump at first which is followed by a laugh.

"That doesn't even look real," Rosienna says

As they carry on along the track, they notice another dummy dressed as a clown wearing a smile and suddenly feathers fall from the ceiling. They all hold their hands out to try and catch one.

"That's just weird," Conor says aloud

"How are feathers scary?" Lucas asks and the others all look at him in surprise

A few non-scary dummies later the train comes to a stop on the track.

"Is it broken?" Maverick asks

"I'm not sure," Lucas says

They sit there looking around into the darkness when fake fire shoots up on both sides of them, which at first makes them jump but then they laugh as something that they think is supposed to look like a devil appears right in front of them and a fake laugh sounds around them.

"Oh come on" people can't seriously think this is scary," Rosienna says

"Apparently so," Conor says

Our heroes have barely reacted to the fake devil, after a few more moments the train moves on and you can see lights moving around overhead.

"What are those supposed to be?" Lucas asks

"That's a good question," Rosienna replies confused

"My guess is that they're supposed to be ghosts??" Conor questions

The train moves once more and comes to another set of small double doors which open and then a very obviously fake skeleton falls from the other side. None of our heroes are scared by this as the plastic skeleton is bent in places and definitely looks fake. as the ride comes to a stop nobody says anything, and it's as though disappointment is in the air.

"Well, what an adventure that was," Rosie says enthusiastically like she really loved the ghost train. "I's could definitely go on that again" they all look back at the smiling dog, giving her a look as if to say you can't be serious, "That was the best ride I've ever been on"

Our heroes all sit for a minute before climbing down and out of the kart laughing

"Now let's go on those rockets," Maverick tells his friends

"Ohh I don't know," Rosienna says "I think I'll sit this one out, it does look really fast!"

"I'm with Rosienna," Lucas tells them "It's too fast for me"

They stand and watch as Conor and Maverick make their way towards the rockets, the rockets are all different colours, with big black numbers on the sides, they choose number twenty-three which is red, with the writing "WHOOSH" down the side of the rocket, when they get in the ride lights up in the most beautiful colours. Lucas, Rosienna, and Rosie all stand watching as their friends whizz around on the ride,

"Look," Lucas says pointing "The man riding the rocket in the middle is going around" and they watch as the little man sat upon the fake rocket in the centre goes around.

"They must be going super fast now," Rosienna says as she watches Maverick and Conor pass them wearing their biggest smiles

When the ride finally comes to a stop, Conor and Maverick jump out of their rocket with a wobble and make their way back to their friends.

"I'm hungry," Maverick says

"I could eat a whole horse....I'm so hungry" Conor tells them

"Be careful what you wish for Mr Conor" Rosie tells him and he gives her a confused look

"I would just like a drink," Rosienna tells them as they walk away from the ride the next riders jump into the rockets

"I need a hotdog," Lucas says

"Ooooo me too, I love a sausage," Maverick says

"Comes with me," Rosie tells them all

She walks them away from the rocket ride and towards where the dodgems are with our heroes closely following, she then stops when she comes to a food stall, where their cooking hotdogs, fries, and burgers.

 The woman standing in the food stall looks really pleased to see them. She pushes her greasy blonde hair back from her face and our heroes notice that she's got a lot of grease on her clothes.

"Ohh isn't your dog, just so adorable," she tells them in a whine

"Yeah we love her," Lucas replies

"And so you should, it's nice to give a dog a home, isn't it," she tells them in a London accent

"It is, We love her very much," Rosienna tells her mirroring Lucas's words

"That's it keeps those compliments coming," Rosie says quietly so only our heroes can hear and it makes them all smile.

"What can I get for ya?" the woman asks them

Everyone seems to panic

"But Rosie we have no money," Rosienna whispers to Rosie

"You order…. I'll sort payment or if you wants yous could's use your feathers," Rosie tells them

"But we can't not in front of her and we need to pay her, Rosie," Conor tells her

"Conor, can you's touch the back of my collar?"

"This is no time for a scratch behind the ears Rosie," Conor tells her

"No… I knows that yous justs needs to touch behind my collar"

He does as she asks and a small pouch appears from the back of her collar where he's just pressed.

"There is money in there, Checks if you's do not believes me's," Rosie says

He opens the pouch and sees lots of old vintage coins.

"Those are all called tuppence, shillings, half-penny's, and cents, you can buy things here with that, you can buy whatevers yous needs or likes, I have plenty more," Rosie tells them

The skinny curly-haired woman on the stall look's back at our heroes, "What can I get you?" she repeats

"I'll have three hotdogs," Maverick tells her

"I believe there is a word I'd like to hear at the end of that young man"

"Oh…yes …please,"

"I would really like a hotdog and some of those sweets please," Lucas tells her. "Oh and another hot dog please, so two please," Lucas says looking down at Rosie who gives him a wink

"A burger and hotdog for me please," Conor says

"And I would like some fries, some candy floss please and a banana milkshake please," Rosienna says

"That will be eight shillings please," she tells them as she holds out her hand to receive the money "Or Maybe we could do a deal?"

"A deal?" Conor asks, "What kind of deal?"

"Well, I'd also like to give a dog a home… if you catch my drift…..."

"I'm sorry I don't know what you mean," Conor says to the woman now feeling confused

"Well….how about I give you ya food…. And…. you give me your little furry friend there?"

"No," they all say

"She'd have a pretty decent home with me" the woman continues

"I already have a pretty decent home...Thanks....plus I don't want to be anywhere near those greasy hands of yours" Rosie says so that only our heroes can hear her

"She's not for sale," Conor tells her sternly

"Everything's got a price, deary," the woman says looking at her

"We wouldn't sell her for all the money in the world," Rosienna says

"She's our dog," Lucas states

"Okay....Okay....." she puts her hands up in defeat "Well that'll be eight shillings please"

Conor grabs a handful of coins from the pouch and holds out his hand for her to take what she needs but she does leave him with nine other coins in his hand, she looks surprised that someone of his age has so much money and seems confused because he cannot hand her the correct amount.

They all stand and wait for their food, keen to get away from this stall and this weird woman, and look around the fairground, it's really busy now. there are people everywhere and the lights all around the fairground are lit up in the most beautiful colours and the sky above is shades of purple and pink with white fluffy clouds dotted through it.

Once their food arrives our heroes seem grateful but they quickly walk away from the weird lady that's asked to buy Rosie – there's definitely something weird about her if you ask me - they find a small patch of grass beside the big wheel and all share something with Rosie and it's almost like a magic trick as the food quickly disappears.

"Ohhh, can we go on the big wheel now…..pleaseeee?" Rosienna asks "Can we, can we, can we,"

"Absolutely," Rosie tells her as she finishes the hot dog Lucas has just given her.

They all make their way towards the big white wheel and stand in line with Lucas still finishing his food as they queue.

"I wills waits heres for yous, I cannots comes on this ones as I am very much afraid's of heights and I fear the conductor wills tells us off if I try and gets on this," Rosie tells them

She sits and watches as our heroes climb into one of the Ferris wheel seats and the conductor places the metal bar down in front of them. But little do our heroes know that they are now being watched from the food stall they were just at - who was that woman and why does she want Rosie so badly?

The ride slowly and gracefully glides to the top and you get to see the most spectacular view of the fairground, it's beautiful and our heroes point out where they have already been and what they've seen and where they haven't been, but I must say it does look pretty awesome to see all the rides lit up and working from this height, and I guess this is almost how a bird would see it.

A few moments later the ride has come back down to the ground and has slowly come to a stop and our heroes climb back out and look for Rosie.... But to their surprise, she's nowhere to be seen, our heroes frantically look around the fairground calling for her.

"Rosie"

"Rosie where are you?"

"Stop hiding will you.... It's not funny" they say between them

"Hang on, something feels wrong" Conor finally says

"What do you mean?" Maverick asks

"Think about it, Rosie wouldn't just disappear would she?" Conor says

"No, she wouldn't just leave us here," Lucas says

"But where could she have gone?" Rosienna asks

"I think the question is why would she leave us?"

"I'm not sure, but that woman back there did seem a bit weird though don't you think?" Conor says

"Yes and she wanted to buy Rosie," Maverick says

"And don't you think that's just a little weird" Conor asks

"I'd say it's a lot weird," Lucas says and you can see panic and realisation that's now across their faces "You don't think she's taken Rosie...Do you?"

"I don't know…. But I don't trust that woman" Conor replies

"What are we going to do?" Rosienna says

"We can't even leave here," Lucas says "I'm not leaving without Rosie"

"I just want to go home," Maverick says as he starts to cry

"It's okay Maverick all we need to do is find Rosie and then we can go home," Rosienna says as she puts an arm around Maverick

"But we're stuck here" Maverick continues "I want to see my Nana Sharon"

That's when they suddenly hear it.

"Will you all be quiet nows" and they're all shocked into silence

"What was that?" Conor says

"It's me…. Rosie" they hear a whispered voice

"Rosie but where are you?" Lucas asks, "Are you okay?"

"How are you talking to us," Maverick asks "I can hear you but I can't see you"

"That doesn't matter nows…. I needs yous to listens to me's very carefully's…. and I needs yous to do somethings very important's for me's" Rosie tells them

"Okay," Rosienna says

"I hasn't's got much times…. I needs yous to splits into twos…. yous needs to makes….. your ways towards the yellow tent, we has…… we has a problem," they hear Rosie's voice say

"What?…. But why?…. Rosie where are you?" Lucas asks

"That doesn't matters" She quickly and quietly replies in a whisper

"Then how are you talking to us," Maverick asks her

"Looks downs at your wrists," Rosie says

They all do as they're told and they notice that the watches are all lit up blue once more.

"Okays, now yous needs to splits up and finds the yellow tent with the red flag on tops…..I hasn't got much times, I'll….." and her voice cuts off

"Rosie??" Conor says "She's gone… we need to find that tent"

Suddenly there full of worry and then they all do as they're told Maverick goes with Rosienna and they turn left in search of the tent and Conor and Lucas go together turning right to see if they can also find the tent.

"Remember what I said" they hear Rosie's faint voice through the watches once more "Not everyone here is your friend……"

Chapter Nine
The Helter Skelter

Rosienna and Maverick make their way through the large crowd and in the direction of what they think is the yellow tent that Rosie had just told them about.

When they get halfway through, they can't help but notice a young boy in a cap, his clothes are dirty, which in turn matches his dirty face and he looks as though he's around the same age as Rosienna, he seems to be selling the largest multi-coloured balloons in all the fairground.

"BALLOONS, COME GET YOUR BALLOONS HERE...WE'VE GOT HEARTS, WE'VE GOT ANIMALS FROM NEAR AND FAR... WE'VE GOT

RED ONES, BLUE ONES, YELLOW ONES, AND GREEN ONES….COME ON BOYS AND GIRLS…GET YOU'RE BALLOONS HEREEEEE" he yells.

Maverick and Rosienna stop for a moment as the young chap stops yelling about his balloons and turns to look at them.

"Can I interest ya both in a balloon? They're the best in all the fairground…won't find no better" he asks them before trying to hand Maverick one and Rosienna quickly swats his hand away.

"Umm…. no thank you…. umm we're looking for the yellow tent with the red flag on the top, you don't happen to know where we can find it do you?" Rosienna asks

"Ahhh…. Yes….. you must mean, the tent of the clowns" he replies "It's ahhh, just over there in that direction" he points behind them and slightly to the right.

Maverick nods frantically and tries to look past the crowd and in the direction of where the young boy has just pointed.

"Just over there…." he repeats pointing once more "I'm Ernest by the way" he continues as he holds out his hand ready for Maverick to shake.

Rosienna quickly swats it away once more

"uhh nice to meet you, Ernest," Maverick says with a smile as he looks at Rosienna but you can tell that she's a little more wary of this boy – I mean they don't know who he is, he could be dangerous or horrible, should they really trust him?

"I can take ya there if you like?" he says in a kind of smug tone as he sucks on the pink hard-boiled sweet in his mouth

"Umm…no…thank you" Rosienna replies as she gives him a look of disgust, watching the sweet dancing around his mouth.

"No honest… it's no bother…. none at all" he replies looking at the two of them.

Rosienna turns and looks at Maverick who's smiling and nodding "That would be very…."

Rosienna coughs and then leans in closer to Maverick "Remember what Rosie said about people here…they're not all our friends" she whispers to him and then answers Ernest…..

"That's very kind of you… but we're okay…umm… thank you…" Maverick tells him and you can see the look of disappointment on Ernst's face.

"We want to explore the fair anyway," Rosienna says before he can object or insist. "Thank you for your help," Rosienna continues with her best fake smile that doesn't quite reach her eyes.

Waving goodbye and thanking him once more, Maverick and Rosienna walk away from Ernest and in the direction that he pointed in.

"If you ever need help…. or a balloon you know where I am!!!" he yells after them

Our heroes just look back, nod and wave at him, before they carry on walking into the crowd till he's out of sight and once more they can hear him yelling about balloons. Maverick turns to look at Rosienna.

"Hang on…. what if he's lying…. and it's a trap?" he asks

"Yeah, maybe your right….maybe we should just double-check that we're going in the right direction… you know to be sure" Rosienna says as she stops and looks around them

"But how are we going to do that? Maverick asks her

Rosienna stands there looking around them

"I have an idea," she tells him "We need to get somewhere high,"

She continues to look around, looking up high above them when she spots something in the short distance.

"I know…we will have to get on the Helter-Skelter," she tells him

As she points towards the ride, with a red twisty long slide going around and around the outside of a wooden-shaped cone, that's been painted red and white, which has lights flashing all the way around and a fancy sign that reads in large letters "The Helter Skelter"

"The what?"

"The Helter-Skelter...look that thing there," Rosienna says as she turns Maverick around and points at the ride, they can see that this ride is fairly busy and full of people of all ages but they mostly notice the amount of children surrounding it.

Maverick looks at Rosienna "That looks fun, lets go!!!" he tells her with a wide smile

They make their way towards it and notice that there are loads of food stalls surrounding it. They continue to climb up the stairs to the top of the Helter-Skelter, and when they've reached it, they can see the whole of the fairground, they notice the rides are all alight in all their glory, flashing different colours of green, white, yellow, orange, pink and blue, and they can't help but notice that there are so many people here. The sun looks as though it's just starting to set in the west, making it easier for our heroes to make out the colours of the tents, carts, and wagons in the short distance, but as they continue to look around their surroundings, a rude, young, blonde, stocky boy comes up behind them.

He stands there for a few moments huffing and tapping his feet before saying "Go dummy" aggressively to Rosienna who's at the front of the queue still looking in the direction of the tents, carts and wagons trying to figure out which one is yellow, she ignores his rudeness and continues to look around.

"GO DUMMY!" the boy finally shouts at her.

"Hey…. who do you think you're calling dummy," she asks

"YOU!"

"Well, your just a rude little boy aren't you! If you're not nice then I'm not moving anywhere" she tells him "Not until you apologise to me"

"You better move!! You're holding up the line" he whines

Rosienna looks behind him "There's no one else behind you!" she tells him in a cross tone "Be patient"

"MOVE….Stupid little girl or I'll make you move"

Maverick frantically looks around trying to spot the tent and you can tell he's now feeling cross with the way this horrible little boy has spoken to Rosienna and that's when she loses her temper

"I WILL NOT! I have just as much right to be here as you do Moron!!" she tells him and you can tell she's really cross now and you can tell the young boy is confused by her calling him a moron.

"Maybe you should just go in front" Maverick suggests to the rude boy as he moves back out of the way with Rosienna to let him past.

The young boy pushes past them both and nudges Rosienna's shoulder as he goes in front of her, but as he goes to stand at the top of the slide she sticks her foot out and he falls head first down the slide with a bang and a very girly scream, this makes Rosienna and Maverick laugh and then high five each other – something they always do when they work as a team and just over her shoulder is where he spots it.

"Look there!!!... I see it!!" Maverick finally says pointing to the right of the fairground and to their surprise the yellow tent really is a bright yellow with a red flag flickering on top, it kind of stands out more than the rest of them and is amongst one cart, two wagons, two steam trains and lots more tents.

"Let's go," Rosienna tells him as she makes her own way down the slide with Maverick following. When they reach the bottom, the horrible little boy is sitting on the floor rubbing his leg and crying saying "Mother, Ohh Mother, I fell down the slide"

Rosienna and Maverick give him a look of disgust and walk straight passed him and in the direction of the tent, as they do Maverick turns to Rosienna.

"I really do hope Lucas and Conor are okay"

Chapter Ten
The Yellow Tent

We find Lucas and Conor standing around the coconut shy, there are people absolutely everywhere, families and friends laughing together as they try to win the games and prizes, like wooden trains and dolls, wooden figures, teddies, as well as sweets and a few ball games.

"Lucas come on we mustn't dawdle and we've got to stick together," Conor tells him as Lucas slowly walks behind him.

"Sorry, there's just so much to see and you know how much I love to play a game" he replies with a huff "I just want to play one or two….. or maybe just even a few of them…just look at all those prizes"

"Can you see it anywhere?" Conor asks Lucas

"No," Lucas says in a glum tone "Couldn't we just ask someone"

"Hmm…I don't know…Rosie said to try and stay hidden, Plus she said to be wary of people we don't know as we don't know who to trust or who's nice"

"This is silly, We've been walking for ages…. and we've got nowhere… where is Rosie? …. plus my legs are tired and my feet hurt,"

"Lucas, can I ask you something?"

"Yeah"

Conor looks around them "Do you think you could…. Umm…. Do you think you could play that game just over there?" he asks as he points back at the coconut shy

"Yeah!" Lucas says as the excitement fills him and you can see his face light up

"And that's how I know your legs are not tired, come on, the quicker we can find Rosie, the quicker we can find out what's going on,"

Lucas and Conor walk a little further when they come across around twenty tents all in different shapes, colours, and sizes, that all seem to be pretty close together, as well as wooden carts and wagons, that

look as though they have come off the train tracks in the short distance.

Looking around our heroes can't help but notice all the people dressed up, people dressed as clowns, men in suits and trilby's, a couple of clowns on stilts, so high that they tower above Conor and Lucas, the strong man that they saw in the circus tent they were in earlier, they watch him lifting weights for a few minutes and even some men dressed as barbershop quartets, in red and white striped waistcoats and white shirts, black trousers and straw hats, practising singing their songs, the sight makes Conor smile - I personally also think it's such a nice and peaceful sound, that instantly makes people smile when they hear it - There are women that are dressed in the most exquisite dresses, you know…showgirls and dancers in dresses that are made out of hundreds of beads and gems, others made out of lace, they notice three dancers in white frilly, knee length dresses and matching hats, standing there practising their routine and singing their songs. two trapeze artists walk out in front of our heroes, while others walk across a long wired type rope above them. In the distance Lucas notices the beautiful horses eating grass in the field, they're white and brown and look so peaceful and not at all like they belong in a place like this, but they do seem reasonably calm, almost like they're used to this.

They spot Tom Thumb who could be mistaken for a child sitting on the steps of one of the carts playing cards with a clown, but he's dressed like a military man and in the distance, you can see a man and his terrier dog doing tricks. As they walk a little further they spot an extremely hairy man and a woman with a beard, whom they recognise from the circus, to be the dog boy and the bearded lady, who both appear in the doorway of one of the carts – we notice that there's a poster on the side of it that says "Dog boy" and a picture of the very hairy man upon it. Walking a little further along, they see the animals in their cages, the two lions and the elephants all in two's sitting behind the barred cages as two men feed them., as well as the tiny monkey from the circus too.

"This must be it, I...I think we're here" Conor tells Lucas and Lucas nods speechless at all the sights before him.

Our heroes make their way through all the talented artists and are amazed by what they're all doing, they notice a fire-breather is in the field behind the tents away from everyone else practising his routine - I mean that's probably the best place for him, I wouldn't like to be too close…. You know getting caught on fire doesn't seem like much fun and I don't think our heroes would be too keen on this either…. you know it might be rather hot and our heroes might get hurt.

Conor and Lucas hurry past him and as they pass the large green tent on the right, and walk around the corner, they spot the very one that they've been looking for, just at the edge of the field just before a row of trees, there it is in front of them the large yellow tent with a large red flag flying from the top, there are carts and wagons surrounding it but there seems to be not many people around it.

As they get closer our heroes can't help but notice that there's a plump, funny-dressed man standing outside the entrance of the tent, in his red and black suit jacket, black, tall top hat and he's holding a long black cane with a golden, shiny knob on the end of it.

"Good day to you young sirs" he calls to Conor and Lucas

"Umm, good day to you too, umm…Sir" Conor replies

"What makes you come over here, you know members of the public don't usually come into our camp,"

"We…We were just looking for someone" Conor replies as they walk past the yellow tent.

"Ahhh, I see…..looking for someone…uhh huh….So tell me….are you looking for the one they call…." And he drops his voice down to a whisper "The one they call Floof?" he asks them in a hushed tone and Conor and Lucas suddenly turn back around to look at him as if a little confused "Also, goes by the name of Rosie?" he continues to whisper.

"YES!" Lucas tells him and the ringmaster looks a little curious and Conor gives Lucas a look with a frown, almost as though he's a tad cross but Lucas realises maybe I shouldn't have told the ringmaster that.

"There is no need to shout young man," the ringmaster laughs a bellowing laugh and they notice that some of the performers that are around them turn and stare at him before carrying on with their tasks.

"Oh…Yes…I'm sorry…I didn't mean to shout" Lucas says looking a tad embarrassed now

"Did you say, Rosie?" Conor asks again

"I certainly did young man"

"Where….where is she?" Conor asks him "Is she okay?"

"She's fine….Just fine"

"Where is she?" Conor asks again, feeling slightly anxious now

"Well come on inside and see," the ringmaster tells them as he walks forward to pull open the front of the tent, he lifts the side of it revealing a small amount of the inside, allowing them to enter.

"Umm… we would love to but we are waiting for our friends….I mean they should be here any minute now," Conor tells him as he then turns to look at Lucas, feeling slightly worried.

I mean who is this man?

What does he want with our heroes?

Does he really know where Rosie is?

And do you readers, think we can trust him?

"Ahhh…and what do those dear friends of yours look like?" his bellowing voice says and Conor can't help but notice how this mans moustache is moving up and down like a black, hairy caterpillar on his top lip.

"Well, Rosienna, she's a girl…. and is very beautiful…. and she has blonde hair….. and Maverick…."

"He's a boy," Lucas says very fast and butting in

"He's rather funny….with red hair," Conor tells him "About this height," he says holding up his hand

"Ahhh yes….don't you worry….don't you worry at all… We'll keep an eye open for them and bring them to you, I'm sure they'll want to see Rosie too…don't you worry yourselves now…in you go… in you go now,"

"Oh…Okay… Well…Thank you" Conor tells him feeling grateful and now feeling a little at ease, and without a look back Lucas and Conor make their way inside the yellow tent.

Chapter Eleven
Danger

Inside it is the most unusual scene, with fire burning in the oil lamps, like candles, that light up the room, an old wooden dressing table sits to the right of the room with lots of little glass pots and china jars, that I can only assume is little like face paints and make-up, and an oval mirror sits on top of it too. An old wooden wardrobe sits to the left of the room and there is a large red and yellow rug covering the whole of the floor, as well as a few wooden cases, some larger than others, which our heroes assume are for some sort of magic trick or maybe they contain costumes or props.

"Have a seat, have a seat," the ringmaster tells them gesturing towards the wooden chairs that are just to the right of the old dressing table and some behind them by the exit to the tent

"Umm….Thank you," Conor says again

"Just you wait here a moment…I'll…umm…. be right back with some drinks…. and let me see if I can find some grub for you to nibble on"

And just like that, the ringmaster walks back out of the tent so that Conor and Lucas are left sitting alone, in the weird room.

"He seems helpful," Lucas says

"Hmm, yes but there's something about him that I'm not sure about"

"What do you mean?"

"He just seems a little odd don't you think?"

"I think he just wants to welcome us" Lucas replies

"Hmm….can you see Rosie anywhere? I'm sure she told us to come here," Conor whispers

"No…I can't…I'm not sure where she is," Lucas replies in another whisper

"Maybe if we call her name she'll come and find us," Conor suggests and they start to do just that

"Rosie" Lucas whispers

"Rosie," they each say again

"Floof" Lucas says and Conor shoots him a look as if to say you have not just called her that silly name

"Rosie…Stop messing around" Conor finally says

"Rosie, are you h.....?" Lucas asks before cutting off his sentence as they can hear heavy footsteps walking towards them and before our heroes know it the ringmaster has re-entered the room holding two cups of water and two containers of popcorn, they watch as he says nothing and walks across the room to place them on the dressing table beside them, his steps make a loud sound as he goes

Boom … Boom….Boom…Boom.

"Uh….Excuse me Mr Ringmaster, I didn't get your name but you said Rosie was in here but we can't seem to spot her anywhere," Lucas questions him

"Just a minute, LARRY!!!" he bellows and with that, the opening of the tent opens once more and one of the clowns comes in holding none other than Rosie who's stuck behind bars in a big black metal cage, she's looking at our heroes and they can tell she's feeling really down almost like she knows she's in trouble, and they can't help her but the one thing our heroes do notice is that Rosie can't look at them and puts her head down so that she's looking at the floor.

"Hey!! why is she in that cage…. and where's her collar?" Conor asks and you can hear the anger in his voice now

"Well it's right here of course," the ringmaster says as he holds out the collar that still has the lights off, he spins it around his finger.

"Hey!! that's Rosie's, not yours" Lucas says "you shouldn't touch things that aren't yours you know"

"It is now," the ringmaster says with an evil laugh "Finders Keepers, losers weepers"

"I think we all know you didn't just find that," Conor says

"Give it back now!" Lucas tells him

"No you'll have to make me" he replies

And much to everyone's surprise, Lucas gets up from his chair and runs towards the ringmaster and kicks him hard on the shins, which causes him to topple forward. Lucas then tries to grab the collar but it's no use, the ringmaster has picked Lucas up with one arm and carries him to the nearest chair and starts to tie a rope around him, Conor runs up behind him and tries to pull him away from Lucas but it's no use, from nowhere two more clowns have appeared, and the clown Larry that has Rosie in the cage has put her on the floor and made his way towards Conor too, who is putting up a good fight against the ringmaster and two other clowns. But it's no good our heroes both find themselves pinned to the chairs once more, with Rosie at their feet.

"Good Luck getting out of that," the ringmaster says with another, evil laugh as he twirls the collar around in his hand and the clowns laugh too, "Come on Barry, Harry, and Larry"

Who are now standing in front of our heroes looking like there evil, Barry is a weird looking clown dressed all in yellow and is plump in size with the brightest orange hair you have ever seen and his face paint is very bizarre, almost as if he's wearing a confused smile, Harry, is an ultra skinny clown that is wearing the weirdest eyebrow's that I have ever seen, that have clearly been drawn on and are halfway up his forehead, the red nose on his face has weird googly eyes on it and angry eyebrows too and he's wearing a white outfit with red and yellow polka dots all over it and the last clown Larry who was holding Rosie, is wearing a bright orange suit and a very sad face that's been painted on his face – he seems very weird as though he can't speak and almost as if he doesn't want to be there. They all one by one leave our heroes sitting in the tent alone, tied to the chairs.

"What are we going to do now? We're stuck" Lucas asks Conor

"I have an idea…but I really hope Maverick and Rosienna get here quickly" Conor says

And as if in the nick of time Rosienna and Maverick carefully enter the tent.

"Lucas, Conor, what are you doing?" Maverick asks

"Stop messing around," Rosienna says "We've got to find this pocket wat….. Hang on where's Rosie?"

"Down there," Conor and Lucas say in unison as Maverick walks around them helping untie them both

"We were just hiding outside," Maverick says "We heard most of what happened"

"Hey Rose, how did you end up in there?" Rosienna asks her and Rosie just looks up at her looking gloomy

"She hasn't said a word since we found her," Lucas says

"Are you okay Rosie?" Rosienna asks her and she just looks at her "Are you hurt or is there something wrong?"

Rosie starts to wag her tail as the others make their way around her.

"Are you hurt?" Conor asks and Rosie lays back down

"Hang on…you can't talk to us anymore" Maverick states

And Rosie stands back up, gives a single bark, and wags her tail.

"You can't talk to us without your collar can you?" Lucas asks as he also realises and tries to open the cage she's in.

She barks again and wags her tail more, then she does a twirl in the cage, Conor manages to open it using a pair of plyers, which he found in one of the drawers in the dressing table, and then she sits on the floor in front of Conor.

"She wants you to do something?" Lucas says

"What do you want?" Conor asks as he bends down beside her, this makes Rosie push up against him, which makes him fall back on his bottom. Rosie then pushes her way onto his lap and places her head on the hand that has the time watch on.

"I'm sorry Rosie…but I don't understand, is it just a cuddle you need?" he asks

Rosie then starts pawing at his hand and the time watch

"She needs you to press it?" Lucas says and Rosie barks

He does as Rosie's suggested and it lights up before their eyes, when the others hold out their hands they can't help but notice the others have now lit up too…. and are now bleeping for some reason.

"What does this mean Rosie?" Conor asks

Maybe she wants us to follow the bleeping?" Rosienna says and Rosie barks and it's as if she's smiling at them with her tongue out.

"But what about the ringmaster and the clowns?" Lucas asks, "Won't they hear the beeping coming?"

At this comment, Rosie sits down and places her paws on her head

"I don't think they will because you have to be wearing one of these to hear it right Rosie?" Conor states and Rosie barks again

"But they're so much bigger than we are," Lucas says

"We've handled worse, remember Billy Jones and Vincent Dale and that horrible girl Phoebe," Conor says

At this memory, Lucas remembers what actually happened with Billy, Vincent, and Phoebe and a smile starts to spread across his face

"Okay," Lucas says feeling braver than normal "Let's go find that collar"

Chapter Twelve
The First Pocket Watch

Our heroes make their way out of the tent and back out to where the performers all were, but to our heroes' surprise it's only just dark out and the sun has finally disappeared, the only lights are from the fairground lights and the bright moon, which are lighting their way. There aren't many performers around anymore either, it's weird to see almost as though the fairground has been abandoned, Conor reaches into his pocket and takes out the bag of the healer, then reaches inside of it.

"God... it's like a cave in here" he tells them but then he feels what he's been looking for and pulls his hand back out and the rest of our heroes can see exactly what he's holding...it's the white feather he holds it between both hands and closes his eyes and right in front of them as if like magic a backpack has appeared, Conor then bends down to retrieve it, opens the zip on it and then he walks towards Rosie picking her up and placing her inside of it, she lets out a long groan but soon settles down within the bag with only her head poking out the top between the two zips on either side of it.

"It will be safer in here for you Rosie," he tells her as he scratches behind her ears and does the bag up a little more so she's safe and not going to fall out. "We don't want to lose you again do we" he continues

She huffs at him and it makes them all laugh because it's almost as if they can understand that she's not at all too happy about this.

Rosienna starts to look around in the darkness through the fairground, she looks a little confused.

"What is it?" Lucas asks

"Can't anyone else hear it?" Rosienna asks now serious

"Umm…yes…" Maverick tells her

"Can you?" she turns to face him and he looks at the floor

"No…I can't" I was joking

"Then you shouldn't say you can then Maverick should you" Rosienna replies

Maverick nods at her, but our heroes all stand and listen intently for the sound of the beeping.

Conor lifts his hand to scratch his face "Hang on…. I can hear it" he says

"How?" Lucas asks

"I don't really know" he replies

Lucas runs his hands through his hair "Hang on me too…I can hear it too"

"But how?" Maverick asks "I can't hear anything"

They stand there silent for a few moments looking around them as they concentrate on listening for the sound.

"Hang on," Conor says as he puts his hands up to his face once more "It's the watches, put your watch near your ears"

Rosienna, Lucas, and Maverick all do as he's told them.

"I can hear it!!" Maverick tells them

"So that's where it's coming from," Rosienna says

"So…It's like a tracker?" Lucas questions

"I guess so," Conor tells them "I'm guessing that if one of us ever gets lost then we can easily be found because Rosie's collar connects to these," he says looking down at his wrist once more "Is that right Rosie?"

Rosie gives a little bark from the backpack which is still on the floor in front of him.

"But how will we find her collar?" Lucas asks

"My guess is that the beeping will become quicker the closer we get to it" and once more Rosie gives another bark to confirm "Okay let's do this" Conor tells them "Let's get that collar back and find that pocket watch,

then we can go home"

Our heroes make their way through the hustle and bustle of the crowds, Rosie in the backpack on Conor's back– and I know what you're thinking it's dark so surely people would have gone home by now, you would think so wouldn't you....but you don't know how wrong you are, there seems to be more and more people here. As we look around we can see people....men, women and children that are laughing and having the time of their lives, and there are small children unaccompanied by their parents running around with various cuddly toys, prizes, and food items. There are circus performers around everywhere, they spot the fire blower who's just to their left doing his fire tricks, obviously, there are a lot of ooooohhhh's and aaaaahhhh's,

The clown's on large stilts towers above everyone and seems to be coming this way and there's a show going on up on the stage where there are the barber shop quartets singing loudly and proudly.

"Can you see them?" Rosienna asks

"No…but I can hear the beeping" Lucas says

"Which means we must be getting closer," Conor tells them "We must stay in the crowd, out of sight, they mustn't find us.

Now, unbeknown to our heroes, Lucas has been carefully looking around at the fairground games and of course the rides. He looks longingly at them and wants to play them more than anything, they walk a little further and they pass the merry go-round and the Helter Skelter once more, which are surrounded by stalls, our heroes stop and watch the rides for a few seconds. When suddenly Lucas turns to his friends

"Look!!.... I've found it!.... I can't believe I've found it"

"Where?" Rosienna asks

"There….Look over there," he tells them excitedly

"The collar?" Maverick asks

"No….no…. look it's the pocket watch…look, It's just over there," he says again and you can tell he's extremely excited by this.

Conor, Maverick, and Rosienna look where Lucas is pointing and just to the left of the merry-go-round and a little further back from it is a small stall, as our heroes make their way towards it they notice that it's a shooting game, and you would need to hit the targets down to win a prize. When they look a little closer they can't help but notice too, that sitting on the back shelve is none other than the pocket watch that they desire, it's very pretty and made of gold and has a long gold chain too, its engraving is very ornate but just as they approach the stall, the watches on their wrists start going berserk and frantically beeping.

"We need to go get Rosie's collar, we must be close," Conor says

"But we can't leave now, We need that pocket watch," Rosienna says looking at the others "that's the whole reason we came here, right?"

"She's right you know, we can't just leave it here now we've found it, what if someone else wins it and takes it, then we'll never find it again," Maverick says

"But how will we get it?" Rosienna asks

"We'll have to win it," Lucas says

"But what if we lose?" Maverick asks

"We won't," Lucas says

"How do you know?" Rosienna says

"Well, who do we know who's the most competitive…. and the best person at games?….. apart from me that is"

They all turn and look up at Conor and then all say

"CONOR"

Conor looks at them all with their pleading faces

"Oh no… I'm not doing it….I can't…..I mean what if I lose? Can't we just see if he'll let us buy it?"

"But you won't lose," Lucas says "You never do"

"It's a shooting game, I kind of have to make sure I hit the targets," Conor says

"And you will….you're better than anyone I know at it," Rosienna says

"You've never even seen me shoot," Conor says

"But I have," Lucas says beside him "And you taught me well…. I mean I've never seen anyone take out Mrs Wilson with water bombs just like you did back home"

And they all smile and Conor starts to laugh looking rather proud of himself

"And I've never seen anyone shoot that nerfs gun at those birds in the garden like you did and actually hit them," Maverick tells him with a wide smile and you can tell he remembers the memory fondly.

Conor looks at his three friends all standing in a row in front of him and he can't help but smile at their pleading faces all standing in front of him, suddenly Rosie barks and it's as if she agrees with our heroes and it makes them all laugh.

'Couldn't we just offer to buy it?" Conor asks his friends again "It would be so much easier"

'I don't think the man will sell it," Maverick says

'Plus we don't have any money anymore, it was all in Rosie's collar.

'I have a few coins left," Conor sighs as he holds out his hand"

'I don't think it'll be enough" Rosienna tells him "But it looks like it'll be enough for one go"

Conor's shoulders drop and he knows what he has to do. "Ahhh …. Okay …okay, I'll give it my best shot, but if I miss it's on you all of you and I don't know what we'll do if I miss"

Conor places the backpack containing Rosie on the floor in front of his friends and walks up to the stall, where the very skinny man with a black moustache and a straw hat on his head is shouting "COME ON BOYS AND GIRLS, WIN A PRIZE EVERY TIME….DON'T BE SHY…. ROLL UP, ROLL UP!!"

'I would like a go please," Conor says to him

"That'll be half a penny, young man"

Conor hands him the coin that has half a penny written on it and the man hands him 5 small pellets

"Ever shoot before boy?"

"Only a few times, but that was back at home…and I've never shot a proper gun before…not like this" Conor tells him nervously

"Ahhh…well the trick is to hold your breath when you pull the trigger… but don't pass out I don't need any more of that today," the man says with a wink

Conor nods, feeling nervous as the man places the first pellet in the gun before handing it to him.

"So I need to get all four of those people-shaped targets down up there?" Conor points

"That's all you have to do son"

"Okay, thanks for the help," Conor tells him as he looks behind at his friends, who all give him a subtle thumbs up

Conor does as the man has told him he leans up on the wooden ledge of the stall with the gun and aims at the first metal man in the row, our heroes watch as he takes a deep breath in and then exhales, he aims and slowly pulls the trigger.

"BANG" "POOF" is the next noise we hear.

"Ooohh, and that's a miss!" the man shouts which really annoys Conor who's now feeling very frustrated indeed, he gives the gun back to the man who re-loads it and hands it back to him almost instantly.

Conor aims once more but just as he's about to pull the trigger he holds his breath,

'BANG, TING"

Maverick's voice is the one we hear from behind him which says "HE HIT IT!!!!"

"YES" Rosienna and Lucas shout, And this makes Conor smile

"1 DOWN" the man shouts

Conor once again hands back the gun and the man reloads it before handing it back to him

"BANG TING"

"2 DOWN!" the man shouts

"BANG TING"

"AND THAT'S THREE DOWN!!!!"

Conor stands there on his last shot, he aims at the last metal man and his arm starts to shake as he's holding the gun, the nerves start to take over, and he's worrying that he won't make the shot, he holds his breath and.....

"BANG TING"

"THAT'S FOUR HITS!!!!" The man shouts

You can hear a cheer from all around them, when Conor turns around he can see the cheers and smiles of his friends, a bark from Rosie, as well as the cheers of the people that are gathered around them, Conor turns back around to look at the man, he's wearing a big smile that's now matching Conor's

"A very well done to you young Sir not many have been able to do that….So, tell me what will your prize be young Sir" he asks

"Umm…I'd really like the pocket watch up on the shelf there please"

"Fine choice for a fine young Sir," the man tells him as he hands him his prize,

As Conor walks back to his friends as he reaches inside his pocket to get the bag of the healer ready to place the pocket watch safe inside of it, but just as he places the healer's bag back in his trouser pocket, our heroes notice a quick sudden movement towards them.

You can see the panic on our hero's faces, as they can see the clowns coming towards them and they all look at Conor who has now picked the backpack up containing Rosie…..

"QUICK…..RUN" Conor shouts

Chapter Thirteen
Ernest

Our heroes run right through the crowds as they notice three clowns and a very skinny, ugly-looking woman catching up with them, that looks as though she was the woman from the food stall where they got their food only a few hours ago – you know the one who tried to buy Rosie - Our heroes run in and out of the rides and the stalls frantically trying to get away and hide.

"Should we go on the rides?" Lucas asks

"NO," they all say

"This is hardly the time for rides Lucas," Rosienna says as they continue to run in and out of the rides

"Hang on….I have an idea, follow me," Lucas says. "I'm serious follow me"

They all follow Lucas towards the centre of the fairground where the circus tent is and where they can see all the rides, they run a little further, first forward and then they quickly turn left, and then right, and right in front of them is none other than the ghost train, everyone seems so surprised that of all places that Lucas has decided to bring them all back here.

"Come on", Lucas says in a hurried tone as he jumps in a kart "They'll never find us in here

The others all look at him with a puzzled expression and then they look at each other – as if to say who is this guy and what have you done with the Lucas that we know?

-You see Lucas used to be so scared of everything, he was always the first to cry, when he was hurt, embarrassed, scared, or angry, he was scared of most things and his friends used to always fight his battles for him, so this was totally out of character for him.

Our heroes take one more look behind them and follow Lucas into the green kart, the ride starts to move along the track with a clicking noise, but just as they go through the double doors again Maverick turns to look at Lucas, who's now beside him, with Rosienna, Rosie and Conor sat behind them.

"Hang on…I thought you didn't like scary things," Maverick says

"This isn't scary anymore," He tells his friends "Their only dummies and nothing to be scared of"

The ghost train goes along just like it did last time, after a while, it comes to a stop at the other end and everything seems really quiet apart from the bad effects of the ghost train making the odd noise and the sound of the clicking along the track as the kart moves along it. when they finally stop when there at the other end, they jump off the train and they can't help but notice how weirdly quiet and empty the fairground has become, it's got dark now and they can't see any people, no people having fun or any performers anywhere.

"Where has everyone gone?" Rosienna asks as she looks around them "Surely we weren't that long on the train"

"I…I don't know" Conor says "Maybe they've closed for the night"

They walk forward a little more and they notice that in the distance the only lights around the fairground are from candle light's that are now dotted around, but it looks as though there are more of them up by the wagons, all the people seem to have gone home, no happy, smiling or even laughing people around anymore and to be honest the fairground does look rather eerie, now that its all turned off.

"We should be really quiet and careful here," Rosienna whispers "We don't know who's around"

"It does look a little odd in the dark doesn't it," Lucas says

"Can't we just go home," Maverick moans

"We can't," Lucas tells them "We can't go anywhere until we've got Rosie's collar back," and Rosie lets out a little groan

"But where can we find it? Maverick asks as they all continue forward

That's when they hear voices as they pass the rockets, and they all move to hide in between two green tents, looking at each other they know what they have to do, they all lift their hands to their ear and they can hear the weird beeping noise again from the watches but this time it seems to be going slightly faster

"Is it me or does it seem quicker and a little louder this time," Rosienna asks

"I was just thinking the same thing," Conor tells them

"Maybe it's near?" Lucas whispers to them

"Maybe we should split up and look for it," Maverick tells them

He and the other two boys turn to walk away from each other but Rosienna stops them

'No!, We should stay together, that's what the letter said remember," Rosienna tells the boys "and were stronger together"

'And that didn't really work out very well for us last time," Lucas says looking at Conor who instantly nods in agreement

'We need to stay together isn't that right Rosie," and Rosie lets out a soft bark in response

Our heroes find themselves spending the next half an hour walking around the empty fairground, talking in low whispers, it's become really eerie now because it's dark and all the rides are turned off and they can't see anyone around. It's late.

How late I hear you ask?

Well late enough for the stars to be twinkling up above and late enough for Lucas to think he can see something in the shadows but when they get closer they realise it's just a funny-looking tree …. Or is it? I would assume that all the performers are fast asleep already, getting the rest they need for the following day's performance, Our heroes start to feel extremely tired, I mean they have been walking for hours.

"Maybe we could just sit down here, you know rest our eyes?" Lucas asks his friends

"I think that's a great idea," Maverick says with a yawn as he drags his feet

"But we can't stop now," Rosienna says also with a yawn "We have to find that collar, and the fairground might be leaving in the morning and we'll miss our chance"

"Shhh….." Conor says pointing to a young boy sat on the steps to the wagon "You need to be quiet, look,"

We watch as Ernest moves sleepily from the step and stands up and walks over towards a bucket of water.

"Hey… that's Ernest" Maverick says

"Who?" Conor and Lucas ask at the same time

"Ernest, he sells balloons and he tried to help us find Rosie," Maverick says "Well, that was before Rosienna kept swatting his hand away, she said we shouldn't trust him"

"But why is he walking around so late?" Lucas asks

"I don't know… but I like him ….we're friends," Maverick says

"No, you are not," Rosienna tells them

"But maybe he could help us," Conor says

"Yeah maybe he could" Maverick repeats

And before we know it Maverick has made his way over to him ready for a conversation before anyone can stop him.

'Hey, Ernest….remember me?" Maverick says

'Oh…umm…hey…Yeah, you were wit that girl that kept hitting ma and away…. She was a real beauty though… she can it ma and away any day she likes" he says and you can hear the sniggered laughs from Conor and Lucas, "What ya doin here so late? Don't yer's Ave an ome to go to?"

'We're lost….a……" he continues

'A Necklace" Rosienna buts in and emerges from the darkness with Lucas and Conor behind her

'We were wondering if you could help us find it?" Conor asks

"Oh, you all ere late are yer, mus be some necklace" Ernest replies "I means I could elps yeah….but what's in it for me?"

'What would you like?" Lucas asks

'Well, a young man like me self likes gold, but there ain't much of that around at the minute," he says "but I do like yer at, he says looking at Lucas"

'You can have it," Lucas says taking it off and handing it to him

Ernest looks down at Lucas's feet and then back up to his face.

'And it as been such a long time since I as had a decent pair of shoes" he continues

Lucas looks at his friends and then very carefully takes off his shoes before handing them to Ernest.

"And I might need so of that money you offered; you know for a balloon"

"but we didn't offer you any money," Rosienna says

"Ahhh, I think you did....if you want me elp that is...." Ernest says

Rosienna looks at Conor and he digs into his pocket and hands Ernest his last remaining coins.

"Right then, what we looking for?" Ernest asks

"Well, we last saw our necklace with some clowns...." Maverick says

"Clowns, you say?"

And our heroes all nod

"And you tried the tent of clowns?"

"That's why we're in this mess," Rosienna says

"They took our....umm.... Mothers...necklace when we got to the tent of clowns," Maverick says

"uhuh, I see," Ernest says

"I think I know where your necklace is then, did these clowns as names, by any chance?"

"Ummm....yes..... one was called Harry....but I can't remember the rest," Conor says

"Barry and Larry" Lucas tells them

"Ahhh yes I know them, not nice characters, not very pleasant either, yep, I'll elp you,"

"Thank you"

"but one last request," Ernest says

"yes??" Conor says

"She has to say she's sorry and give me a kiss"

"what no!" Rosienna protests

"Well no deal then," Ernest says as he folds his arms over his chest

"Rosienna, just on the cheek is all you have to do," Lucas tells her

"Come on," Maverick says

"I'm not doing it….you can't make me"

"Well that's fine… see you around… the fair leaves at 5 am," Ernest says as he goes to walk away, waving at our heroes.

"Rosienna come on," Lucas says

"Come on Rosienna, take one for the team"

"it'll take 1 second"

"FINE," she says and you can tell she is furious "she stomps towards him and stands in front of him "Just one kiss and then you'll help us,"

"That's what I said treacle"

"Fine," she says and you can tell she's really mad now "I am not your treacle, so don't call me that! I don't like it"

"Alright Darlin," he tells her as he holds his hands up

"Whoa… I am not your Darlin either" she bites and he looks shocked at her rage which is written all over her face.

Rosienna leans forward and kisses Ernest on the cheek and his cheeks glow bright red.

"Happy now?" she asks

"and I think you were going to apologise for hitting me"

"No chance"

"Then no elp," he says

"I'm sorry," She says through gritted teeth

"That's better, I'll elp you… follow me…this way"

And they follow him into the darkness and you can hear sniggers from the boys

"You are to never mention this again, do you hear me," Rosienna says "And you owe me big"

And you can hear three "yes's" in the dark as they continue to follow Ernest.

Chapter Fourteen
The Collar

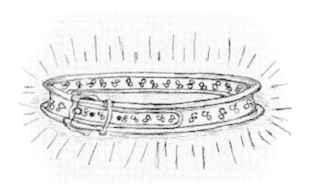

Suddenly a noise that's become rather familiar to them startles our heroes and the watches on their wrists start to beep incredibly fast, bringing their focus on finding the collar, they have followed Ernest through the fairground and towards some tents hidden away from the other wagons and fairground rides and in behind the huge circus tent is a smaller one, this one looks as though its seen better days and has small rips in the sides, as well as the left side seems to look as though it's leaning a lot. As they get closer that's when they hear them.

They turn and look at Ernest who starts to speak in a whisper

"This is where…I ahhh leave you"

"Thank you," Conor says

"Yes thank you," Maverick says

"That's okay... I hope you find your necklace and you know where to find me little lady" he says tipping his new hat towards Rosienna who looks at him in disgust as he disappears in the dark once more. As the voice of a man bellows and echoes around the night air and through the valleys.

"HAHAHAHAHAHA, Harry you did very well good fellow, very well indeed, I couldn't have done it better myself," He yells and you can hear a slapping on the back and I can only assume he's slapped him in the shoulder to express his gratitude towards the clowns.

"Well Harold,....Harold...Harold, I know you would have done the same for me, and now we can take that collar and collect those pocket watches from all over the realm of time,"

"WE CAN, WE CAN" Harold who actually turns out to be the ringmaster says nodding before picking his bottle up and taking a sip from his drink

"Don't you think you've had enough Harold?" the whiny voice of the woman says from inside the tent

"DON'T YOU TELL ME WHAT TO DO WOMAN, I'LL DRINK WHAT I LIKE, DON'T YOU KNOW US MEN ARE THE SUPERIOR RACE, it says so throughout time I'll have you know"

And the three clowns all laugh at his words while she stoops back towards the tent she was in only moments ago

"WHILE YOU'RE IN THERE WOMAN GET US ALL ANOTHER BEER" he yells again and you can hear her muttering to herself in a cross tone. "She did this last time we tried to get all those pocket watches you know, the boss was not impressed, now this is our final chance to success Harry, the boss won't accept failure again, that young girl took it from us last time, do you remember"

"How could I forget," Harry says glumly "I've only just stopped hearing about it"

"It's him," Lucas says as he stands there watching them clink their bottles together again and it's as if they're celebrating something.

"It's who?" Rosienna whispers

"It's the Ringmaster and the three clowns Harry, Barry, and Larry…but I'm not sure who THAT woman is," he says pointing toward her

"That's the women from the hotdog place," Rosienna says "but who are they all? And why are they here?"

"They were the ones that stole Rosie," Conor whispers

"And her collar….and they even tided us to chairs," Lucas tells them in a hushed tone

"We need to get her collar and then we can get out of here," Conor tells them

"But I don't understand who they are or why they're here?" Rosienna says

"But where is her collar?" Maverick asks

"I can't see it," Conor says

Rosienna looks down at her watch on her wrist "I have an idea she tells them and they all watch as she gently taps the watch strap twice, a wide, smug grin spreads across her face as she watches as it starts to slightly light up blue again but this time it's very dim. She then makes her way around the tent but she stays hidden

"Stay there," she tells them and then she's back in seconds, "So, do you want the good news or the bad?" she asks

"The good" Lucas whispers in a jolly tone

"Well the good thing is, I found Rosie's collar" and you can see Rosie getting excited from the backpack

"And the bad?" Maverick asks

"The bad thing….. is that it's inside their tent"

"But how will we get it from in there, they're all sat outside the front and that women's in there," Maverick says

"It's impossible," Lucas tells them

"No…. it's not" Conor interrupts "all we need is a distraction"

Our heroes spend the next half an hour making a plan a little way away from the tent in which the collar is in, they whisper to one another and a short time later they all know what they have to do. Maverick is the brave one that has decided he wants to joke with the ringmaster and the three clowns and thinks maybe that's the best way to get Rosie's collar. He takes his feather out of his pocket and wishes for dirty old clothes from 1925, he then covers his face in mud with the use of a large muddy puddle that's not far from the tent, with the help of Conor and Rosienna. While Lucas uses his white feather to make his wish, which is for a pair of trainers and three pairs of sharp scissors which suddenly appear in front of them, he hands each of the scissors to Rosienna and Conor before taking one for himself.

"Right are we all clear on what we need to do?" Conor asks

"Yep"

"Yes"

"Yeah"

"Okay then Maverick get ready and we will wait for your signal, Lucas and Rosienna you need to go and get in position"

They do as Conor has told them, Conor stands just around the side of the tent and the ringmaster and the clowns are all sitting outside still laughing and discussing their plan to steal all the pocket watches. Conor looks at Rosienna and Lucas who each give him a thumbs up and then to Maverick who does the same and gives Conor a thumbs up in return.

We watch as Maverick walks around the side of the tent so he's in full view of the Ringmaster and the three clowns and he starts to fake cry.

"Hhhhave yyyyyyou seennnnn Mamaaaa?" He asks them "I hhhhave lost myyyyy Mamaaaa" he cries

"I'm afraid not son, what does she look like?" the ringmaster says

"Don't you think it's late for you to be wandering around on your own?" the clown called Harry asks

"But... iiiiii cantttt finddd my Mamaaaaa," Maverick says again

Just then the ugly woman comes running out from the tent, her hair is brown and extremely curly and almost like a bush, her nose is big and crooked and her eyes are huge, she's dressed in a long dirty, floor-length dress and you can visibly see her bones around her back, and she looks like she's in need of a big, good meal.

"Ohhh Sweet boy please don't cry; We will help you find your Mother…just you come inside and tell Margaret what she looks like and I'll see if I can help find her"

You can hear Maverick's fake sobs from inside the tent, "I don't know where she's gone" he says "she's left me here" he cries "I miss my Mama….have you seen herrrrr"

"HAROLD!!!!" the woman yells "HAROLD!!! YOU GET YOURSELF IN HERE NOW, WE NEED TO HELP THIS LITTLE LAD FIND HIS MOTHER"

"Ohhh god woman you're sticking your nose in other people's business again" he yells back to her "The lad will be just fine on his own and find his way home eventually or his mother will come back for him," he says as he gets up and walks towards the tent, once inside we hear him shout once more, "HARRY, LARRY GET YOURSELVES IN HERE, I NEED YOUR HELP!!!"

The rest of our heroes watch as the clowns all follow Harold the ringmaster into the tent each of them moaning as they enter.

When our heroes are certain that there all inside you here Conor shout

"NOW"

Quickly, he, Lucas and Rosienna run around cutting the strings that are holding the tent up, they watch as it slowly starts to go down, engulfing the clowns, the Ringmaster the woman and Maverick within the tent.

"Maverick?" Lucas says feeling worried a minute goes by and there's still no sign of him

"Where is he?" Rosienna says

"Give him a minute," Conor tells them

And with that, they watch as Maverick climbs out of the tent holding Rosie's glowing collar and then running towards them.

"Quick, get it on her" Rosienna says as Maverick runs and hands it to Conor who instantly puts it on her.

"Ahhh that's is betters" they hear Rosie say

"Rosie," they all say giving her a cuddle as Conor takes her out of the backpack.

"We better get out of here," Conor says

"How do we get home Rosie?" Maverick asks

"Ahh, it is so goods to be back, we get homes with the balloons of course's," she says calmly

Conor reaches into the bag pack of the healer and pulls out an orange balloon and hands it to Lucas.

"Lucas you brought us hear now take us home"

And the next thing our heroes know is, Rosie's collar has lit up and so have the watches and with a "POP" of the Balloon a bright white light shines and then everything around them goes very dark.

Chapter Fifteen

We're Back!!!

Our heroes find themselves back in the tent that they were in what feels like days or even weeks go, laying upon the colourful cushions once more.

"We're back," Maverick says "I mean that was fun and all but those clowns were really scary…. and that woman kind of looked like a witch"

Rosie turns to look at our heroes who are laying among the cushions.

"Well that's was such an adventure…" Rosie says

"I guess you could call it that Rosie," Conor says

"Who were those people?" Rosienna asks

"They's were the bad guys"

"But why do they want your collar so much?"

"So theys can travel through time to find the watches and use them for evils"

"We know that Rosie but why?" Conor asks

"Because what is contained in these watches have magnificents powers, stronger than any human or animals," Rosie tells them "Only the Violet witch can uses them for whats they is intendeds"

"I thought they were going to get me there for a second" Maverick says

"Yes Maverick that was a very brave thing you did back there," Rosienna tells him

"Yes thank yous Maverick, Very braves very braves indeed"

"You should have seen them all up close, they were hideous, and her nose was huge" he states

"Conor I has to ask, Do you has it?" Rosie asks him

They all watch as he reaches into his pocket and pulls out the bag of the healer, followed by the pocket watch they've retrieved.

The pocket watch is solid gold, with the most ornate engraving around the outside and the infinity sign engraved into the back, the chain is thick gold and it looks sturdy, almost as though its originally come from the year 1925 – I mean it has…just now…. but where was it originally made I wonder and why - it is now also glowing a blue, just like the watches on their wrists and Rosie's collar,

"Wow," Lucas says

"look at that" Rosienna says

"It's so pretty," Maverick says

"It is, indeed, now Conor yous musts holds on to its, so it is safe's in the bag of the healer, only the four of yous can open it"

He nods and places it back in the bag, before safely passing it to Rosienna

"But I guess the only question left to ask is…. Rosienna where are we going on our next adventure……..?"

Where will our heroes go next?

Will they find the next pocket watch?

And can they really trust everyone they meet?

Now I know you all have so many questions, but you'll just have to wait until next time to find the answers.........

About the Author

Hi,

Thanks for purchasing my first children's book!

I hope you've enjoyed reading it just as much as I have enjoyed writing it.

If you haven't read already, my name is Sophia-Rose, I'm from a small countryside village in Cornwall, in the United Kingdom.

I'm just your normal, average girl who has big dreams. I live with my young son, my partner and our dog, who has been my inspiration to this book and sat by my side every step of the way as I've created this world, this book is a series of 4 so look out for my other books coming soon.

I also want to thank the children in my life for inspiring this story and im delighted that they now have their very own story, so I dedicate this book to them.

Look out for my next book coming soon out April 2023

Best Wishes

Sophia-Rose Lucas

Sophia-Rose

Printed in Great Britain
by Amazon